Dawn *of* Day

J.A. McPhail
illustrated by **Gwen Battis**

Rowe Publishing
and Design

ISBN 13: 978-0-9851196-1-4
ISBN 10: 0-9851196-1-6

1 3 5 7 9 8 6 4 2

Printed in the United States of America
Published by

Rowe Publishing
and Design

www.rowepublishingdesign.com
Stockton, Kansas

This book is dedicated to
the original pioneer families of
Wabaunsee, Kansas, the Beecher
Bible and Rifle Company of 1856,
and their descendents who have
kept their story alive.

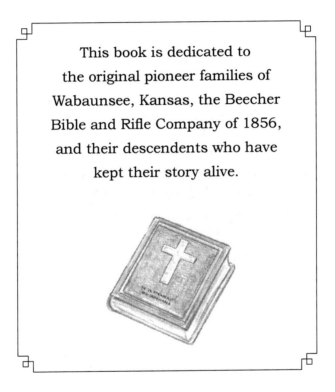

ACKNOWLEDGMENTS AND THANKS

To my dad, Arlie V. Aadalen, who taught me to love books, libraries, and museums—and stopped to read all historical markers.

To my mom, Irma Jean Willig Aadalen, who encouraged me to write—especially about the history of her childhood home in Wabaunsee.

To my big brother Dave Aadalen, who helped me grow up, and is now my lawyer.

To my wonderful husband, Dennis McPhail, who supports me in everything I do, and works hard teaching, counseling, and coaching, so I can stay home and write.

To our amazing daughter, Stacie, who's always in my corner, and is the joy of our lives.

To five generations of Willigs, and the historical and spiritual heritage you passed on to me.

To Roy Bird, who mentored me throughout my years at the Silver Lake Library and stayed on the job as one of my Kansas history experts, writing coach, and freelance editor.

To Michael Stubbs, an amazing expert on Kansas and especially Wabaunsee County history. The historical quality of this book would not have been possible without the time and effort you so generously provided during my research and editing.

To Jane Miracle Goeckler, who recommended me for my job at the library, and shared her family history which holds the same Wabaunsee County heritage as mine.

To my friends at Silver Lake Library; being your director was the best job I ever had.

To Cindy, Ashley, Amber, Amy, Lauren, Garrett, Justin, Melissa, and Marjorie, for reading my first draft, liking it, and encouraging me to keep writing.

To Kathryn Mitchell Buster and Carol Cook, for invaluable help with stories and the history of the Mitchell family.

To my dear friends, John and Marjorie Oathout, for driving me all over the Kansas territory to take photos and learn more about all the places in this book; and singing together for 23 years.

To the Morganton Writers Group—Carol, Debra, Georgia, Gwen, Linda, Maggie, and Terri—for your tireless help, advice, encouragement, and amazing editing skills. You ladies rock.

To Gwen Battis, illustrator extraordinaire; I am so glad God put us together.

To Sherri, at Rowe Publishing and Design; for your expertise and believing in this book.

And to my Heavenly Father, who is still worshipped today at the Beecher Bible and Rifle Church in Wabaunsee, Kansas; I give You all the praise and glory.

CONTENTS

PART ONE

Henrietta's Story: Bibles, Rifles and a Painting

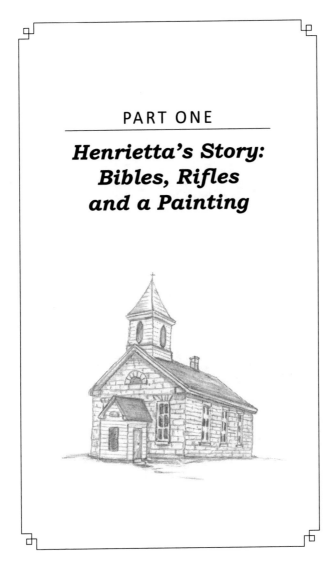

CHAPTER 1

The Story of the Old Stone Church

Wabaunsee, Kansas, August 26, 1932

"You best git yourself back here," I hollered, "and ride beside me like Mama said!"

Irma Jean rounded the corner by the Old Stone Church, pulled hard on the reins and brought Trixie to a halt. She grinned and waved in my direction then stuck out her tongue. She slipped off her pony's bare back and tossed the bridle reins over the hitching post.

"Come *on*, slowpoke," she sang at me as I pulled up beside Trixie.

My little sister is six years old and hates it when Mama asks me to watch her, but our parents won't let her go riding alone.

Irma Jean skipped across the churchyard, her short blonde hair bouncing in time with her dancing cowboy boots. I dismounted, tied up my horse, and brushed the dust from my dungarees. Mama had pulled my own mop of sandy hair firmly back in a stubby pony tail, but I tucked a few strays behind my ears. I followed Irma Jean over to the big locust tree where our neighbor sat in front of her easel.

"Hi, Maude!" Irma Jean greeted her. "Whatcha paintin'?"

"Well, good morning, Irma Jean, Henrietta." Maude reached over and gave us each a quick hug. She removed her wire-rimmed glasses and wiped the lenses on the hem of her flowered dress. After replacing them on her face, she patted her silver curls and adjusted her paint-spattered smock. "I'm painting a picture of the church for Old Settler's Day on Sunday. What do you think?"

"Mmm, that's nice." Irma Jean's blue eyes slipped across the canvas and landed on Maude's face. "But you know that picture you painted for us, Maude, the one of Grandma and Grandpa's ol' stone house? Well, Daddy hung it over our fireplace and it sure looks good. You even put my climbin' tree in it!"

She plopped on the ground and pulled off her boots. Irma Jean went barefoot whenever she could get away with it.

"Irma Jean," I scolded, "you should call her Miss Mitchell." She turned to me and her face scrunched up, which meant "you're not my mother." "Don't give me that look," I told her firmly. "I'm almost thirteen and it is the older sisters' job to teach you some manners when Mama's not around. When I was your age, Myra taught me things like that. Only I was much easier to teach than you are."

A smile spread across Maude's face. "That's all right, Henrietta. I don't mind you girls calling me Maude." She turned back to my sister. "I'm glad you liked the painting, Irma Jean. I hope to display it in my art show next month if your parents will let me borrow it for a while."

Irma Jean stretched her skinny neck forward and squinted at the painting. She twisted around to look at Maude's horse and wagon, then pointed her finger and said, "Hey, Maude, isn't that your horse, right there?" Thankfully, she pulled her finger back just before it made contact with the fresh paint.

"It certainly is," Maude answered. "You're very observant, young lady." Maude also pointed at a spot on the painting. "And that wagon is the very same one my daddy used when he transported runaway slaves."

"Runaway slaves?" Irma Jean's face scrunched up again. "What's a bunch of slaves got to do with your wagon?"

We heard the front door of the church open and our Aunt Jo appeared. She was pretty tall anyway, but her rigid posture made her seem even taller. There was a good breeze but the starched ash gray dress she wore barely moved as she marched toward us. Her hair matched the color of her dress and was held in place by a nearly invisible hair net. She walked straight and sharp, her shiny black shoes clickity-clacking over the stone path. She pushed her black metal rimmed glasses back up on her nose with a bony finger. Irma Jean raised her chin and cocked her head to one side, giving our aunt her most courageous big girl stare. As usual, Aunt Jo ignored her.

"Are you about done, Maude?" she asked. "Mel wants to take our photograph with the Sharps rifles and the Bible for the photo display."

I sniffed and thought I was going to sneeze. Even Maude's oil paints couldn't overpower the scent of Aunt Jo's stale rose perfume. I pinched my nose, willing the sensation to pass. I'd found it was usually best to avoid Aunt Jo's notice, but I needn't have worried since she ignored me, too. Even though we are blood relatives, Aunt Jo usually never talks to anyone in the family—even Daddy, her own brother. We hardly ever saw her, and that was fine with us girls, because whenever we did, she always acted mad at us even when we hadn't done anything wrong.

"I could definitely use a break," Maude said, standing up and stretching. "Duty calls, girls," Maude continued, "but I promise to tell you about the wagon in a little bit. Don't go away."

I nodded my head. "Sure, Maude."

Maude set her paint pallet on the chair and stuck her paintbrush in a pile of blue goo in the middle of it. Looking down at her wrinkled and smudged painting clothes she added, "I'm not exactly dressed for picture taking, Jo."

"Just remove that thing and you'll pass," Aunt Jo ordered like she was a general inspecting the troops.

Both women stood tall, straight, and eye to eye. But Aunt Jo reminded me of a soldier at attention, while Maude looked like she might once have been a Gibson Girl in one of Mama's catalogs. Maude lifted her hand to her forehead and saluted Aunt Jo, then turned, winked and gave me a grin that plumped her rosy cheeks like a pair of ripe cherries. I tried not to smile since Aunt Jo could still see my face, but it was nice to watch someone who wasn't intimidated by my aunt.

I helped Maude slip out of her smock and she slung it across her chair. Aunt Jo directed her into the church and Irma Jean and I followed them. We tried our best to stay out of the line of sight so maybe Aunt Jo would forget we were there. Several members of the Willing Workers Society were in the front of the sanctuary cleaning and sorting through books, music, and photos.

"Here we are, Mel," Aunt Jo said in her usual commanding way. "You may immortalize us now with that contraption of yours."

Mel stopped working on a pile of music and grabbed his boxy camera. "Why don't you stand out there in the vestibule and I'll get a shot by this table of memorabilia," he told them. "Now then, show me how a woman can handle those old carbines."

Maude and Aunt Jo each picked up one of the guns. I knew Aunt Jo did a lot of hunting with the family when she was younger. She was the only girl in the family and Daddy told us how she always bragged about being as good a shot as her brothers.

I jumped when Irma Jean's elbow delivered a sharp jab to my thigh. She

grabbed my neck and pulled me down to whisper in my ear.

"We best get clear outta here, Sis. Aunt Jo gots a gun!"

I bit my lips to keep from laughing, although I will admit that being in the same room with Aunt Jo and a rifle was scary. We slowly melted into the stairwell leading to the balcony.

"Let's get another photo, please," Mel said, "only this time with one of you holding the Bible." Aunt Jo picked up the big black book, opened it, and showed it to Maude. A second flash from Mel's camera lit up the vestibule. He took one more and then laid his camera down. "Thank you very much, ladies. That's all I need. You can go back to your painting now, Maude."

Maude laid her rifle on the table and stroked the cover of the Bible Aunt Jo put down beside it. "It's hard to believe it's been over seventy-five years since this Bible and rifle arrived from New England with my father," Maude said. "I am so glad when we met on Decoration Day this year, that we decided to form the Old Settlers' Association. Now future generations will always remember why and how this church came to be."

Mama and Daddy had told us a little about the history of the church, but Maude seemed to know more of the story. I wondered what it was.

Aunt Jo and Maude headed outside. Aunt Jo looked back to see if we followed them. She looked like she wanted to say something to Maude that she didn't want me and Irma Jean to hear.

I stopped on the stoop and Irma Jean slipped past me. She disappeared around the corner of the church, making a beeline for the outhouse, the straps of her overalls already flapping loose behind her. I decided to act like I was going along, but once I was out of sight, I backed against the wall and peeked around the corner. I made sure I was still within earshot of Maude and Aunt Jo. I wanted to hear what they had to say.

CHAPTER 2

A Family Secret

"Before you came out to get me for the photographs," Maude said to Aunt Jo, "I was just about to tell the girls how my father hid runaway slaves in our wagon."

Shading her eyes, Maude turned and looked at the bell tower. "I remember when your brother Henry was about Henrietta's age and climbed into the belfry. I was in high school and had the task of watching the older boys' Sunday School class outside after church. I looked up and there was Henry climbing out on the roof! I found out later that he was trying to get a piece of one of the shingles. They were about to replace the roof and since your granddaddy was the one who made the shingles, he wanted to whittle something out of it!" Maude paused and shook her head. "It was a miracle he didn't fall. I hollered at him to get back inside, but his mind was made up. Thank God he got down safely."

"Henry always was determined when he wanted something." Aunt Jo crossed her arms in front of her. "Perhaps that's why he fancied himself in love with one of our hired help and decided to marry her—in spite of how some in the family felt about it."

"Josephine! Hush now," Maude said looking around for us. "Henrietta and Irma Jean might hear you talking about their mother and father like that."

I shifted my weight to my other foot and accidentally stepped on a branch. When it snapped, I ducked back out of sight. The last thing I wanted was to get caught eavesdropping. I sneaked one eyeball just barely beyond the edge of the stone wall, just in time to see Maude place her hands on Aunt Jo's shoulders.

"You need to let it go, Jo. People don't own slaves anymore or white servants either, like Lena and her family. People are paid honest wages for honest work. I don't care what color they are. Your attitude toward Lena isn't any better than the way some masters treated their slaves."

Aunt Jo's mouth squeezed into a thin line.

I leaned back against the church wall. Even though it was a hot day, the stones were cool on this shady side. My mind sifted through what I'd heard. Maybe Mama thought I was too young to

understand. I knew there was something wrong between my parents and Aunt Jo, but nobody ever told me what it was. I don't think Myra even knew the real story and she was already graduated from high school.

Aunt Jo began to speak again. "Father was one of the wealthiest men in Wabaunsee County," she said. "It simply wasn't proper that his son up and married the housemaid. I will never understand how Henry could do such a thing."

I let out the breath I was holding. So this was why Aunt Jo was mad at Mother and Daddy ... and us girls, too. My very own mother was a maid in Grandpa's house when she and Daddy fell in love and got married. It was just like a romance novel!

I heard Irma Jean slam the outhouse door. I caught her arm as she tried to run past me and clapped my hand over her mouth.

"Shhh," I whispered, "be quiet. I want to hear what else Aunt Jo is saying." I guess she could tell I was serious, because she quit squirming. We both popped our heads around the corner of the church. I think Irma Jean thought it was a game, like hide and seek.

"Let's drop this subject, Maude," Aunt Jo continued. "Helping slaves get their freedom was one thing, but Henry marrying Lena was quite another."

Aunt Jo looked at her pendant-watch. "I need to get home. I'll see you tomorrow." She crossed the yard and climbed into her new coupe.

She never looked back, just put the car in gear, and took off down the dirt road. Dust billowed out from under the car marking her path even after she disappeared from sight.

Maude walked over to her horse and stroked her mane. "Don't worry, girl, I'd rather ride and feed you than have to buy gas to ride around in that fancy motorcar of hers."

Irma Jean broke free of my hold and ran around the corner, talking to Maude all the way. "I'm back, Maude. I sure feel better now! Were you looking for us?" She plopped on the ground. "So, are you paintin' that picture of the church for Old Settler's Day on Sunday? You know tomorrow we're all helping the Willing Workers finish fixing things up real nice. And after church on Sunday, we're havin' a picnic right here in the churchyard! I'm already hungry. Boy, you sure do paint good. Can we stay and watch you finish it while you tell us that story 'bout the wagon? I'll keep quiet, I promise." She leaned against the tree trunk, waving me over.

"My goodness, Irma Jean," I said sitting down beside her. "You chatter more than that squirrel up there in the tree. Won't you ever stop?"

"I don't think she will, dear, at least not while she's awake!" Maude laughed and winked at me. "But you both are welcome to stay and watch me paint. I'd love to tell you the story now."

Maude picked up her brush, dipped it in white paint, and then black. She smeared the colors together on her pallet. "By the way, Irma Jean, I saw how you left poor Henrietta in the dust when you two pulled up to the church earlier. You should slow up a little. You're pretty small to be riding so fast."

"I'm three feet and five and a half inches tall! Besides, I'm solid and scrappy, Daddy says."

"That's because she's Daddy's little tomboy," I explained to Maude. "Mama always says her two oldest daughters were born sweet young ladies. But Irma Jean would rather go fishing or hunting or ride the tractor with Daddy than do girlish things."

Irma Jean looked up at me proud as could be. I ruffled her boy-cropped hair and then turned my attention back to Maude's painting. She added another shingle to the church roof with the gray-brown mixture she'd made.

"See here, girls? These shingles I'm painting are like the ones your great-grandpa carved out of wood by hand. All he used was a broad ax and a knife. The folks founded this church in 1857 and finished this building five years later."

"Hey," said Irma Jean, "1857 was seventy-five years ago, wasn't it? That's why we're having a party this Sunday!"

She acted very pleased with herself for figuring it out, but I had a feeling she'd overheard Mama and Myra talking about it.

"Very good, Irma Jean," Maude said. "You'll do well with your numbers when you go to school this fall."

Maude put her brush down, wiped her hands on her paint rag, and brushed a lock of silver hair from her eyes. She turned away from her easel, crossed her ankles, and placed her hands in her lap, giving us her undivided attention.

"How would you girls like to hear the story about how my father became Captain Mitchell of the Prairie Guards?"

Irma Jean didn't act too interested until Maude leaned in close like she was telling a secret and whispered, "He was almost hanged, you know."

"Hanged? Like from a rope? Yes, tell us, please!" Irma Jean clapped her hands together several times. "And don't forget about the wagon."

Maude looked directly in our eyes as she began to speak.

"My father, William Mitchell, was what was known as a conductor on the Underground Railroad and our log cabin was a station house." Maude nodded toward her painting. "That wagon right there carried many runaway slaves to their freedom."

Usually I wouldn't have wanted a history lesson in the summertime. But there was something about Maude's face that made me want to hear more. She looked like a little child, excited to set out on a grand adventure. I settled back to listen as Maude resumed her story.

"It was the spring of 1856. A famous preacher from New York, Rev. Henry Ward Beecher, was the special speaker at a church in Connecticut. My father was in the meeting that day. He'd already agreed to join about seventy other men, and move to the Kansas Territory. Many of them had to leave family, friends, and everything that was familiar to them. But they believed in freedom for all men and that's why they came."

Irma Jean rested her head against my shoulder. She wrapped her hand around the crook of my arm as Maude continued.

"When the Connecticut Kansas Company arrived here in late April, they found some others already settled here, including you girl's great-grandpa John. Together, they founded the town of Wabaunsee. That's a Potawatomi Indian name, and it means exactly how they felt about coming to Kansas. It was a brand new 'Dawn of Day.'"

PART TWO

Maude's Story: They Call it Bleeding Kansas

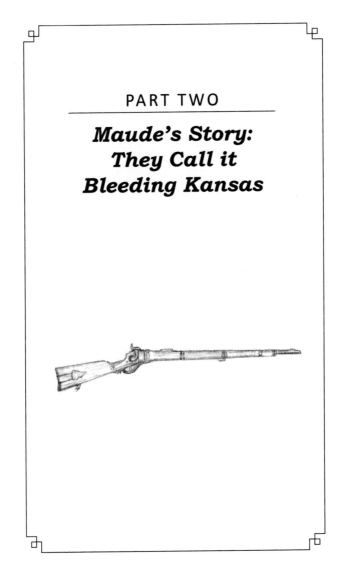

CHAPTER 3

The Connecticut Kansas Company is Born

New Haven, Connecticut, March 22, 1856

The Reverend Henry Ward Beecher strode across the front of the Old North Church. His strong clear voice showed no signs of tiring though he had spoken for almost an hour about his passion to abolish slavery. Preaching from the text found in the Book of Acts, Chapter 10, Reverend Beecher reminded his captivated audience how God sent the Apostle Paul to take the Gospel not only to the Jews, but also to the Gentiles.

With his large black Bible clutched in one hand and a copy of his sister Harriet's book, *Uncle Tom's Cabin*, in the other, Beecher paused to give a last plea. He raised his clean-shaven chin and shook his head, dislodging his dark wavy hair from the collar of his long black waistcoat. His penetrating eyes roamed over those in the congregation, silently imploring them to join his cause.

"I tell you this evening, ladies and gentlemen," Reverend Beecher concluded, "just as Paul learned in this passage of Holy Scripture, God has directed us not to call *any* man common or unclean, whether he be rich, poor, white, or black. For God is no respecter of persons; but in every nation, it is he that fears the Lord and works for His righteous cause who is accepted by Him."

Sitting in the front row was a young man who joined the rest of the crowd in enthusiastic applause as Reverend Beecher returned to his chair next to the pulpit.

William Mitchell's chiseled facial features were framed by his neatly trimmed brown hair and beard. He exuded confidence as his deep-set blue eyes gazed around the room. Noting the crowd's avid support of the Reverend Beecher, a satisfied smile appeared below William's generous mustache. Tall, lean, and muscular, William's carriage and attitude were evidence of his experience and strong capabilities.

Though only thirty-one, William had already sailed around the world. His parents brought him from Scotland, to the village of Middletown, Connecticut, when William was only a year old. He left home when he was twenty-four, arriving back in Connecticut just in time to join this group of men heading west to Kansas. He was proud to be included because they intended to make the territory a free state when it joined the Union. American slavery was the most unjust thing he'd ever witnessed. And William Mitchell knew first hand about injustice.

When William was only a boy, his father told him about the famous *Amistad* trials, which took place just a few miles from Middletown. His father, William Mitchell, Sr., was one of the eleven members of the Middletown Anti-Slavery Society. William would never forget the day his father had taken him to see those African men from the *Amistad* where they were being held in the prison at New Haven. While the courts determined their fate, the prisoners were paraded outside like a circus sideshow. People came from miles around just to gawk at them.

"William," his father told him, "these men are victims of hateful profit-driven men who kidnapped them from their homeland in Africa. They were hunted down, sometimes betrayed by their own people, captured, and treated like animals during the long ocean journey. Packed in the bowels of the ship with little food and water, they arrived in Cuba to be sold as slaves."

After leaving home when he was eighteen, William worked the gold mines on the Feather River in California. William learned that some of the white men made thousands of dollars without lifting a finger to dig for gold. Instead, they hired local Indians to do all the work for them, but refused to pay them a decent wage. The scoundrels just laughed it off and paid them with a few trinkets or a bit of food. The Indians knew no better than to accept it, although William tried to make them understand the value of their labor.

William left California to try his luck in the gold fields of Australia. Thousands of men from other countries joined him in the search for the precious metal. There, it was Chinese immigrants who became the victims of prejudice, many of whom William befriended. These men were viscously teased because they looked different from everyone else. Many times the ignorance of such stupid bigots caused William to stand up and fight for his Chinese friends.

"I have seen many outrages in my travels," William told his father when he finally came back home to America.

"But I cannot stand by and watch as children are ripped from their mothers, thrown on the slave auction block, and sold, never to see each other again. Like you, Father, such atrocities make my blood boil."

Stirred by Beecher's sermon, Charles B. Lines, who had invited the Reverend to speak that evening on the "Kansas Question," stepped forward and addressed the crowd. Charles was a gentle giant, refined, and soft spoken, with deep spiritual convictions.

"I firmly believe that the only way to make Kansas a free state is to settle the land with anti-slavery citizens. I've organized a company of seventy men who are willing and ready to take on that challenge. We've raised funds and the plans for our journey west are set in place."

Taking out a handkerchief, Charles dabbed at his mouth, which was almost hidden in a bushy thatch of six-inch gray whiskers. His grandfatherly face showed a touch of anxiety as he glanced over at Reverend Beecher, picked up a rifle from behind the pulpit, then turned back to the crowd. "My concern now is that although we have most of our provisions, we are going into dangerous

and hostile territory, and we need more weapons like this with which to defend ourselves."

William looked around at the audience as silence settled over the room. He'd been told that with his rugged good looks and outgoing personality he was a "born leader." It was true that dealing with people came naturally to him. Perhaps he would have to put his skills into practice this very evening if the company was going to raise enough money to purchase firearms for their protection. But before William had a chance to stand to his feet, someone in the back jumped up.

"I quite agree, Mr. Lines. And I pledge money for one Sharps rifle!" The shout came from Professor Silliman of Yale University.

"I shall pledge another," a fellow faculty member added.

William lifted his hand into the air. "I pledge the third rifle."

"And I'll make it four," came from a voice across the room, "pledged on behalf of the junior class at Yale University!"

The crowd grew tense, waiting.

"There are times when self-defense is a religious duty." Reverend Beecher rose to his feet again, lifted his arms for effect, and raised his preaching voice. "If that duty was ever imperative it is now, and in Kansas. If this community pledges enough funds for twenty-five rifles, on behalf of my congregation back in Brooklyn, I shall pledge enough for an additional twenty-five Sharps rifles to the Connecticut Kansas Company!"

The crowd came alive. Like popcorn roasted over a campfire, people jumped up to offer their assistance. Soon the number of pledges mounted to twenty-seven rifles—enough to put Reverend Beecher's promise into effect.

William left the meeting very pleased. Money for at least fifty rifles had been pledged by the townspeople and Reverend Beecher. It wouldn't be long now until they would be leaving New England to start a new life in the Kansas Territory. William knew this was the right decision for him. He'd always felt God had given him a spirit of adventure and compassion. He'd learned to use those traits to help his fellow man, wherever he went. Now it was time to go to Kansas.

A few days later, Mr. Lines received $625.00 from the Brooklyn, New York church. Along with money to purchase the rifles, a member of Reverend

Beecher's congregation also sent twenty-five Bibles and hymn books. Beecher's name was not printed anywhere on them, but each of the Bibles had the words "Be Ye Steadfast and Unmovable" printed on the front cover in gold lettering.

A few minutes before midnight on March 31, William gathered with the rest of the company. They were anxious to be on their way. Before the trip ended the colony would travel by steamboat, train, and ox drawn wagon. Five scouts had been sent on ahead to look for the best locations for a new settlement, and the rest of the colony would meet up with them in the city of Lawrence, Kansas. All the travel arrangements had been made and their belongings were already loaded on the steamboat that would take them on the first leg of their journey.

Charles Lines stood in front of the crowd and unfolded a piece of paper. The letter he held had been sent with the money, Bibles, and hymn books. It was from Reverend Beecher.

William rubbed his arm over the goose bumps that had risen there. As Mr. Lines read the message, the group who would soon be known as the Beecher Bible and Rifle Company began to stand up straighter. They were determined and proud to defend their faith and the cause of freedom. They were making history, and with friends and families' promise to pray for them, they were ready to begin their journey. William listened carefully so he wouldn't miss a single word.

◇◇◇◇◇

"Let these arms hang above your doors as the old revolutionary muskets do in many a New England dwelling. May your children in another generation look upon them with pride and say, 'our fathers' courage saved this fair region from blood and slavery.'

We will not forget you. Every morning's breeze shall catch the blessings of our prayers, and roll them westward to your prairie homes. May your sons be large hearted as the heavens above their heads; may your daughters fill the land as the flowers do the prairies, only sweeter and fairer than they.

I am in the bonds of the Gospel and the firm faith of liberty.

Truly yours,
Henry Ward Beecher."

CHAPTER 4

Welcoming Committee at the Free State Hotel

Lawrence, Kansas, April 17, 1856

William looked down the wagon train in front of him, his horse easily cantering past them one by one. Raising his hand in greeting, William slowed his horse to a walk as he came along side Charles Lines' rig.

"So, Charles, we finally reach the town of Lawrence. It has been a long few weeks has it not? But a good trip," he said.

"Yes, it has been good," Charles replied. "God granted fair weather and safety from our enemies. I am grateful we did not encounter the places where violence has already erupted."

"Lawrence is a more populated town than I anticipated," William said looking at the building-lined street. "This must be the main road." He pointed across the street. "That's quite a fine hotel there across the way. Do you think our friends received word that we would be arriving today?"

"I would say they did," Charles answered. "Look there." The two men watched as the front door of the hotel swung open. "It appears we have a welcoming committee." Charles and William rode toward the group gathering in the street ahead. Charles set the brake on his wagon and climbed down as William dismounted.

"Good day, gentlemen," Charles said, extending his hand to the man out front. "We are from New Haven, Connecticut." He smiled. "You probably know us as the Beecher Bible and Rifle Company."

"Ah, yes!" The leader of the welcoming committee shook Charles' hand first and then turned to William. "I am Shalor Eldridge, formerly of Massachusetts, and currently proprietor of the newly opened Lawrence Free State Hotel," he said gesturing toward the building behind him. "We are so pleased you have arrived safe and sound. Please, come in and have some refreshment. I'm sure it has been a long journey for you."

Charles, William, and several of the other men followed Eldridge into the hotel. The aroma of a freshly prepared meal wafted through the air making William's mouth water. Their host was well-dressed and impeccably groomed, obviously a gentleman. He possessed gracious manners and a pleasant expression, the sum of which put William totally at ease.

After the travelers had washed up and enjoyed something to eat and drink, the two groups sat down together to talk.

"We have come to Kansas to settle in this new land and build a place where we can raise our families in freedom and according to our faith," Charles began. "We certainly pledge our assistance in the fight to establish this territory as a free state. In return, any assistance you can offer us would be greatly appreciated."

"Thank you for your pledge to aid our cause. We will do all we can to help you also," Eldridge told the newcomers. "We have heard of a few skirmishes in the past couple of days between the border ruffians and free-state forces. The town has been protected thus far, but the citizens of Lawrence are concerned that more trouble is close at hand."

The conversation continued for awhile but grew quiet when Eldridge stood up and addressed the room.

"Should destruction again threaten our families and our homes, we know that in you we shall find brave hearts and strong arms." The rest of the Lawrence free-staters looked around the room at the men from Connecticut as Eldridge finished. "We are encouraged to know that our strength will be greater, and hence our victory more certain."

Charles replied, "The people back in New England will be happy to hear of your gratitude for the efforts they are making. I am certain more settlers will come. We believe Kansas Territory is where the final contest will be fought to decide whether freedom or slavery shall rule the destiny of this country."

The meeting was over and the two groups parted with handshakes all around. After they had rested a while, Charles and William led the company from Connecticut out of town. Their journey was not yet over.

Three days later, they arrived at their first destination. One of the scouts the company had sent ahead thought Mission Creek would be good for a settlement, but the company decided it was too far off the beaten path. They wanted to be closer to the river so they continued on to Wabaunsee.

◇◇◇◇◇

William was impressed with the stark beauty of the Kansas Flint Hills, so named for the layers of flint rock hidden beneath the mounds of dark rich prairie soil. To the north, smooth and lofty river bluffs ascended beyond the fields across the water. Gently rolling hills bordered the east and west, and waves of tall prairie grass stretched south as far as the eye could see. William was sure Kansas would be a good place to put down roots. But more importantly, the new residents of Wabaunsee could now become voting citizens of the territory. Hopefully their votes would assure Kansas entered the Union as a free state.

Soon after their arrival, William and several of the other members of the company gathered in the afternoon by Antelope Creek. Some of the local settlers joined them to discuss steps needed to formally establish the town.

Charles Lines wanted to make sure one of the first orders of business was to build a church. The locals had been holding services in homes or outdoors when weather permitted. The building of a school was also at the top of their list, as well as establishing businesses in the community.

"Look there, men. We have company." Dr. Joseph Root, a physician and fellow member of the Connecticut company, pointed down the road. Despite Dr. Root's dark wispy hair and beard, his face had a boyish look, which now registered concern. "Someone's riding in fast."

They watched as the man came near. Enveloped in his own dust, he pulled up to the little group of men assembled on the banks of the creek. Dismounting, he dusted off his pants and wiped his face with a kerchief pulled from his back pocket. The newcomer looked to be barely more than a schoolboy. Standing next to Charles Lines he looked even younger, his height not even reaching the shoulders of the older man.

"Good day, gentlemen. I've come from Lawrence to enlist your aid. You said you had able-bodied men willing to help us. We're calling for our allies now. We face a sure attack of proslavery forces and need all the assistance we can gather. Will you make good on your promise to help?"

"Hello, son. I'm Dr. Root. What is your name?"

"Tom Waters. Pleased to meet you, Doctor." Tom pumped Dr. Root's hand as though he hoped to get water from it.

The crease in Dr. Root's forehead deepened as he removed his handkerchief and wiped his forehead and hands. "As you know we only arrived here ourselves two days ago. We have much to do to establish our new homes and community buildings. I'm not certain we can spare many men right away."

"We believe the raiders could attack within the week," Tom said. "I was sent to inform those who pledged to stand with us that they are needed as soon as possible."

William stood up and reached for Tom's hand. "The name's William Mitchell, Tom. Would you mind excusing us for a while? We need to talk this over and decide our best course of action. Please make use of the creek if you'd like. You may cool off and clean up while we discuss this matter."

"Thank you much, I'll do that." Tom headed down stream a bit to give all of them some privacy.

"What do you think, men? We simply can't send a big party right now," said William. "We need to get properly quartered and start building our cabins." He stroked his bearded chin with a sigh. "However, we did agree to help them. And after all, it was for this very reason we came to this land—to abolish slavery and fight against those who support it."

"We all know why we are here," Charles said. "But I think we also agree that it would be too risky to leave the settlement before preparations were made for its care and protection. It wouldn't be fair right now to ask our men to drop all the things they are planning to do to build our town, even for the cause of freedom."

"Gentlemen, if our new friends need our help," said Dr. Root, "I certainly don't want to leave them at the mercy of a band of raiders."

"May I make a suggestion," William interjected. "What if Joseph and I go talk with them again and assess the situation? When we return we can decide what further measures need to be taken."

The others agreed. William and Dr. Root decided to leave as soon as possible to see for themselves how things stood with the Lawrence free-state men.

Tom wandered back to the group, hair slicked back from his wash in the creek. He adjusted his damp hat on his head.

"That felt mighty fine, gentlemen, but I need to be on my way. What do you say, can you help?" Hearing their answer, Tom shook hands with several of the men, thanked them, mounted his horse, and rode toward the next settlement on his mission.

"Just a minute, William." Charles pulled him aside as the meeting broke up. "Would you and Dr. Root mind checking on something while you are gone? Another member of the company is expecting letters from home. His last correspondence said they should have arrived in Lawrence already. Someone there may know where the letters are being held." Charles handed William the papers giving him the authority to pick up the other man's mail. "Be careful, though. Mr. Hart returned from Topeka last night and said proslave forces have been intercepting mail intended for free-staters."

"I'll be glad to pick them up, Charles. Hopefully that report isn't true in this case. But we shall handle it if we run into any trouble." William pocketed the papers and turned to Dr. Root, who'd joined them.

"I believe we should try to make it to Topeka as soon as possible, Joseph," he said. "When we get there, we will leave the team of oxen and the wagon at a stable, hire a couple of mules, and push on. Mules will be faster, easier to find, and cheaper than horses."

◇◇◇◇◇

William and Dr. Root returned to their tents, packed a few belongings for their trip, and were on the road quickly. When they arrived in Topeka and found a stable for the oxen, the owner gave them news.

"A man just arrived here and said ruffians are patrolling all the roads leading in to Lawrence. If you two are heading that way, you'd best keep an eye out."

Not letting the news delay their departure, the two friends headed east following the Kansas River. At Tecumseh, a proslave settlement east of Topeka, William motioned for Joseph to be quiet and follow him.

"I hear horses coming," he whispered. "We should be able to avoid them if we keep to the creek bed and use the brush as cover."

Dr. Root discovered that William excelled at hiding. He followed as silently as he could. Joseph had no desire to get a close look at a border ruffian today.

First one, and then another patrol passed them by brandishing weapons and jugs of corn alcohol. After they had disappeared from view, William stepped out from the trees.

"That was too close for comfort," he said to Joseph. The patrol had been no more than a couple yards from them but remained totally oblivious to the two men in hiding. Thankfully, their mules were quietly grazing a ways down the bank of the river out of sight. "It's a little early for them to be drinking like that," William said, "but I'm glad they were too concerned with their liquor to notice us."

"It is a miracle," Joseph said, "but I do not think they were aware of our presence at all. However, perhaps it would be advantageous to wait until dark to resume our journey."

"I agree," William answered. "Let's make camp in that stand of cottonwoods and bluestem over there by the river. I'll get the mules and we can take turns resting for the remainder of the daylight hours."

◇◇◇◇◇

As the sun started to sink in the west, William and Joseph remounted their mules.

"We will try going cross-country," William said. "If we keep the river in sight we should remain traveling in the right direction. We will stay on the bluffs in the trees instead of on the road. That should bring us to the outskirts of Lawrence by daybreak."

"I'm glad Tom gave good directions," Joseph said several hours later. "We should be there soon. After seeing how many enemy patrols were between here and Topeka, I see why our Lawrence comrades are calling us in already. It seems our friends are going to need all the help they can get."

An hour later, as the sun was just coming up, they located the cabin near Lawrence Tom told them about. The free-state militia men were expecting recruits and were glad to see William and Dr. Root arrive. After introductions were made they all sat down at a table.

"Mr. Mitchell and Dr. Root, we thank you for coming," said the man who had answered the door. "We have seen many bands of proslave forces already gathering together for an assault against the people of Lawrence. They are definitely preparing for an attack."

"Excuse me, but did you say you are a doctor?" One of the other men stepped forward and addressed Joseph. "We have an injured man if you wouldn't mind looking at him."

While Dr. Root treated his new patient, William told the rest of them about their journey of the last twenty-four hours and how they'd seen several bands of ruffians patrolling the area.

"We'll head straight back and get our men together," William told them. "In fact, they are already making advanced preparations." William looked around the room. "First though, we need to find out if some letters for one of our company have arrived here from Connecticut. Do you know where they are being held? Also, is there anyone who can accompany us at least part way back to Wabaunsee? We should use the quickest route and we are not yet familiar with the area. We want to return with all speed, but considering the proslave forces we've already encountered, there is certainly more safety in numbers."

"I will show you where the letters would be if they haven't been confiscated. I also know two men who will be willing to go back with you," their host said.

After the meeting, William and Joseph followed the man into Lawrence to pick up the letters Charles asked them to bring back. They had arrived safely, so

William took them, folded them, and put them inside his boots for safekeeping. He'd learned on his travels that hiding things in his boots was a good way to keep them from falling into wrong hands.

The four men set out on the river road to Topeka that evening. When they were only a couple miles west of Lawrence on the Old California Road, they saw a log cabin just ahead. Through the broken chinking between the logs, William could see light, so he knew the building was occupied. What he didn't know was whether the occupants were friends or enemies.

CHAPTER 5

Arrested!

West of Lawrence, Kansas, May 5, 1856

When the foursome started to pass by, a volley of musket fire was blazed at them through the holes in the chinking. The sound of gunfire startled the horses of the two guides and they bolted into a gallop toward the river. The horses' speed allowed the men from Lawrence to escape. That was the last William and Dr. Root saw of their new companions.

"These must be a couple of those stubborn Missouri mules," William commented dryly to Dr. Root when their own mounts refused to move. It wasn't long before the rifle-bearing party emerged from the cabin and surrounded William and Dr. Root. They were a scraggly bunch, definitely not a trained military unit.

"Dismount and surrender," one of the men instructed. William Mitchell did not like being told what to do, especially by a stranger who looked and smelled like he hadn't had a bath in weeks—except maybe in a tub of whiskey.

William was sure these men couldn't possibly have instructions to delay them personally. He started to protest when the same man interrupted him, his gun carelessly bobbing from his armpit. "If Commander Stringfellow decides you're all right, we'll let you be on your way in the morning."

Dr. Root leaned over and whispered, "William, I think we better do as they say. Since we're new to the territory, nobody will know our names and they'll turn us loose."

William was less willing to give in so easily, but he did as his friend suggested. They dismounted without further protest.

"We'll take your guns and mules for tonight," the filthy man said. "You can have 'em back in the morning if we don't find no warrants for your arrest."

"It is apparent we have already been arrested," William said. They were led to a small hut being used as a guardhouse. Several others were already in custody when William and Joseph entered. The door shut and they heard a scrape as their nasty captors dropped the bar-lock securely into place.

◇◇◇◇◇

The next morning, William and Joseph were awakened at dawn.

"Get up, you new pris'ners. My orders is to escort you one at a time to the Commander for questionin'."

The interrogations didn't take long. When they both returned to the guard hut, William and Joseph relayed to each other what happened in their individual sessions with Commander Benjamin Stringfellow.

"The only question he asked me was if I was sound on the goose, or sympathized with the Free State party," William explained. "When I said 'Yes, Sir, I do,' the guards turned me around and brought me back here."

"It was almost the same with me," Joseph answered, "although I tried not to arouse his wrath by coming right out with it. He stared me down nose to nose, then asked about my political leanings. I told him the reason I came to Kansas was to support the Free State cause, but I assured him I was also looking forward to settling out here on my own land. Still, I don't believe he was any more pleased with my answer than yours." Joseph looked out the small window. "Before they ushered me out, I overheard something you won't like. Stringfellow said to hold us for a couple of days to see what more they can find out about you. They don't like your attitude one bit. He said perhaps you need to be taught what happens to brazen abolitionists around here." Joseph and William both sat down to await their fate. "I wonder what happens now," Joseph concluded.

Later that day, one of the ruffians entered the prisoners' hut and pointed his gun at William, who reclined on a greasy blanket on the dirt floor.

"Hey, you, Mitchell. Stand up," the man demanded. "I'm supposed to search you for some illegal letters you is hidin'."

"Be my guest," William said from his place on the floor. Dr. Root could see his friend was outraged and not about to give in to this slimy man's demand to stand up.

"I was about to engage in an afternoon nap." William stretched his arms above his head, bent his elbows, and locked his fingers beneath his neck. "But conduct your search if you wish." Staring the man in the face he added, "Is there a reason I am being singled out for this special treatment?"

"We got a report from one of our men in Lawrence that you is hiding letters you picked up in town. Now you jest pull off them boots so I can search for them letters. We was told that's where yer hiding 'em."

"Spies, I see." William lifted his leg up. "Pull my boots off yourself if you care to see what's inside, in addition to my foot of course," William replied. Dr. Root rolled his eyes.

The guard reached down and pulled William's boots off one at a time. He turned them upside-down, but shaking them thoroughly, he failed to find any letters or hidden messages of any kind.

"I'm goin' to report to the Commander," the guard said throwing William's boots back at him. He aimed at his chest but William caught the boots in mid-air. He pulled them on and stretched back out on his blanket with a satisfied grin.

"You best git that smirk off your face," the guard hissed as he opened the door. "Maybe I didn't find nothin' but I'm tellin' the Commander you didn't cooperate with the search!" The guard slammed and firmly secured the door behind him.

"Did you have to react like that, William?" Dr. Root shook his head as he walked over to his rumpled blanket lying behind the door. "You only make things harder on yourself, and probably the rest of us," he said as he grabbed the blanket and shook it out. "Where in the world did you hide those letters anyway?"

"They're right here." William lifted the dirty blanket he'd been using for a bed, reached in, and pulled out the three letters. His eyes sparkled even in the cabin shadows. "I decided to believe the reports concerning mail thieves."

The door flew open and knocked Dr. Root against the wall. William jumped to his feet, ready to strike back.

It was obvious the guard had waited outside listening and overheard William say he had the letters. William thought about trying to disarm the man, but the guard stepped toward him, shoved the butt of his rifle into William's chest, and knocked him down. Snatching the letters out of William's hand as he fell, the guard whipped around and exited. The entire encounter happened within seconds.

"Now you will feel Stringfellow's wrath," Dr. Root said as he helped William to his feet. They didn't have long to wait. Several guards returned and William was dragged before the Commander and several members of his band.

"That was not a very intelligent thing to do, Mitchell." Stringfellow's whiskey breath about knocked William over. At first glance, the man's appearance was deceiving. If William had passed Stringfellow on the road when he was sober, he might have thought he was a lawyer, businessman or perhaps a politician. But tonight, the way he was berating both William and his own men, it became clear that whatever he did for a living, Stringfellow was nothing more than a belligerent drunken tyrant.

Stringfellow leaned into William's chest and slurred, "I should just shoot you. But as it happens, we're in need of a cook for my men and all the prisoners. There are fifteen of us and seventeen of you. That will be your responsibility until I say different. Take him to the mess tent and tie him up till it's time to fix supper."

However, when mealtime came, William flatly refused to cook anything for anybody. He was immediately dragged before the Commander once again. By this time Stringfellow and most of the men in his band of ruffians had been drinking heavily and were getting loud and rowdy.

"I would suggest you obtain control over your men, Commander. Your prisoners might escape and leave you all dead in your stupor."

William's words enraged Stringfellow. "That's mighty brave talk for a man in your position, Mitchell." He paused. "I believe it's time to hand you over to my troops. I'm sure you'll learn to keep your mouth shut eventually. Perhaps they may even have a permanent solution."

William watched as one of the ruffians reached for a rope.

CHAPTER 6

"Hang the Abolitionist!"

"Here, I'll do the honors," the man with the rope volunteered.

"Yeah. Hang the abolitionist!" chorused around the room.

The rope was already formed into a noose. The first man threw it over William's head and pulled it tight around his throat.

"Hey, men, looky here, a perfect fit. What you say 'bout that, you slave lover? I don't hear no jabberin' now." The man was so close to William's face that the liquor fumes almost choked him. He resumed his taunting. "What's the matter, boy, you already got a pain in the neck?"

Accompanied by his comrades' laughter, he grabbed William around the waist, while his cronies helped lift and force him to stand on a chair. Next, they extended William's arms and his wrists were tied together in front of him.

"Hold him steady now, mates," the unofficial hangman said. He threw the rope over the rafter above. "Now I just have to pull this here rope tight, kick the chair out from under him, and we

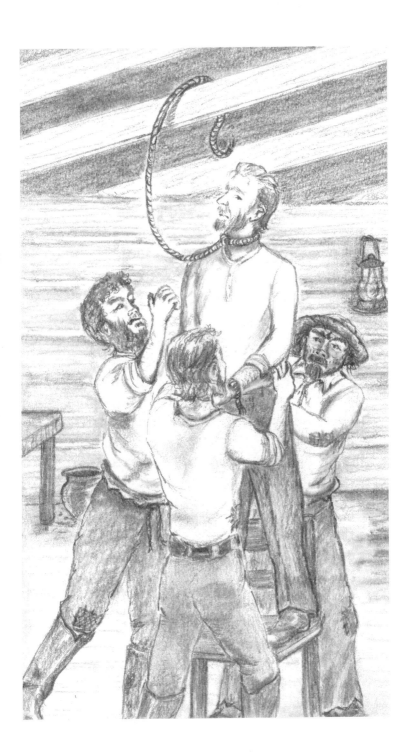

can watch him swing!" The rest of the men cheered, clanking their casks in a death toast. William tried to squirm out of the noose.

"Now what was you sayin' 'bout prisoners escapin'?" Two men who were weaving back and forth approached William, proding him with their earthenware whiskey jugs.

William's eyes flashed and his bound hands balled into fists. "Do you really want to do this?" He glared at his captors. "Then, come on."

Not tying his arms behind his back proved to be a mistake. William reached up and grabbed the rope above the noose, successfully taking the pressure off his neck. Kicking out with his boots, William managed to break two ruffian's demijohns of whiskey just as they were clanking them together in a second toast. The crockery exploded in their hands. Broken shards sliced their hands and they yelped in pain. Golden whiskey, mixed with red blood, flowed from the gashes.

"Why you sorry black heart!" said the man reaching for William. He fell as William's boot lashed out a second time, connecting with his unshaven jaw in a resounding crack. The rest of the ruffians in the room swarmed toward William but hesitated when they came within reach of his dangerous boots. Had they been sober, William would have been in a much graver position. As it was, his confidence grew.

However, William wasn't sure of his next move. He muttered a quick prayer for divine protection and scanned the room for any possible allies. He spotted a teenage boy, sixteen or seventeen, who had just entered the cabin with an older man. The pair surveyed the scene, the older man looking at Stringfellow for an explanation.

The young man watched William for a moment, a curious determination in his eyes. William saw the family resemblance between the two. Perhaps this was a father and son, or two brothers. Both were dressed in the latest New England fashion. The older had silver streaks in his hair and a firm jaw line lending him an aristocratic air. He was as clean-shaven as his younger counterpart and both were close to William's height. The younger man turned to the older one.

"Uncle, aren't you going to help him? It appears these drunkards intend to kill this man."

"I believe you are right, Isaac," the man said with a sigh. "I'll take care of this," he said placing his hand on the boy's arm. "You stay out of the way."

Isaac stood in the doorway watching William as his uncle took a few steps forward.

It was apparent that Isaac's uncle was not pleased with the wild drunken crowd. He seemed almost disgusted at their behavior, but hesitant to interfere. His expression changed as he crossed the room, from non-committal resignation to one possessing an air of authority. He marched over to William, causing the other men to back away.

They were wary of this man's presence. Isaac's uncle commanded a strange control over the room, as though he was truly in charge. Or at the very least, the other men weren't willing to cross him.

"For those of you who are unaware, I am Governor Wilson Shannon and I order you to release this man," he said firmly. "I will not tolerate an unlawful hanging. Does anyone know who he is? What has he done that warrants his death?"

Nobody spoke up. All the men in the room were looking from Stringfellow to the governor. Stringfellow stood in silence.

"If he has a price on his head, he must be turned in to the territorial authorities in Lecompton, alive. I suggest you find out who you are dealing with before you do anything further to his person."

Governor Shannon helped William down, removed the noose, and untied his wrists. Nobody tried to stop him, including Stringfellow. Isaac rushed over to steady the chair as William stepped to the floor.

"Thank you, son," William said as he shook off the ropes.

One of the men, whose hand was still bleeding from William's kick, spoke up. "Look what that scum did to my hand, Gov'ner!"

"That's Governor Shannon to you," Stringfellow interjected, placing his body between the two. The rest of the men broke apart, slinking into the darker corners of the room, several of them mumbling about their fun being ruined.

William certainly wasn't going to question what had just happened. He simply looked heavenward and offered a silent prayer of thanks.

Governor Shannon led William outside, leaving the rest of the men to clean up the mess they'd made during the evening's entertainment. Isaac followed William and the governor out the door.

"I don't know who you are or how you landed yourself in that position, but I know Stringfellow's men were feeling the effects of freely flowing whiskey. I deemed it best to step in on your behalf."

"The name is William Mitchell, Sir, and I am much obliged to you for your interference."

Isaac stepped up beside his uncle. "This is my nephew, Isaac," the governor continued. "He has recently begun the study of law, with the intention of someday joining my brother's law practice in St. Joseph."

Governor Shannon paused to look up at the stars shining above them as if they held the wisdom he needed. "What happened in there this evening?"

"Last week my friend and I were on an errand to Lawrence when we were taken prisoner by these roughnecks and thrown in that guardhouse," William said pointing to the hut which had been their quarters the past several days. "We have done nothing wrong, except I refused to cook for those men and they wanted to string me up because of it. We came with a company from Connecticut, are newly arrived in the territory, and only wish to be about our business of establishing our new homes."

"I see," the governor said with a slight smile. "Perhaps your trouble tonight also had something to do with your stance on Kansas becoming a free state? To tell you the truth, I have had issues with both sides of the question during my term in office. Nonetheless, tonight you and my nephew here have taught me a valuable lesson. Common decency seems in short supply these days."

William knew he'd experienced a miracle. Not only because the territorial governor had been in the camp that evening but also because he managed to keep the drunken crowd from carrying out his hanging.

"Thank you, again, sir," William told his rescuer. Turning, he added, "and thank you, Isaac, for speaking to your uncle on my behalf tonight. You are a courageous and just young man. Excellent traits for a lawyer to be sure."

Governor Shannon was silent a moment. "Yes," he said looking at Isaac. "There are times when young people have better sense than adults." He patted Isaac on the back. "I will see what

I can do to procure you and your friend's release. Now if you will excuse us, Isaac and I need to be on our way." He looked around and spotted a man with a rifle leaning against the cabin.

"Guard!"

The man approached Governor Shannon immediately. "Return this man to his friends," the governor ordered. "Good night, Mr. Mitchell.

Upon entering the guardhouse again, Joseph sprang to William's aide and performed an immediate examination. Much to the doctor's relief, William appeared to have no lasting injuries.

William told his friend about his near death experience and how Governor Shannon and Isaac intervened.

"I thought you were done for," Joseph said gently placing his arm across William's shoulders. "My prayers were answered, my friend. I must say when the good Lord sends help, he goes right to the top, does he not?"

For two more days the men were held in the guardhouse.

The next evening William heard guards talking outside the door of the hut.

"Sheriff Jones is leading a posse into Lawrence tomorrow," one of the guards said. "I heard more from our side are coming from all over, and some groups have already caused a good deal of trouble for the free state men."

"I heard Stringfellow say Atchison will be there and arrests will be made," added another guard. "Serves 'em right. They should all be arrested and hanged!" Their voices trailed off as the group of guards moved on.

No mention was made of Governor Shannon. William assumed he'd left the area. Hopefully, he'd also left instructions for their release and the return of their property.

CHAPTER 7

An Eye-Witness Account

Lawrence, Kansas, May 21, 1856

The next morning the prisoners were awakened early.

"Git up and get in a line, all of you. Take anything you want to keep. We're goin' for a little walk." The guards marched the prisoners out of their hut and up a nearby hill where a frenzied crowd of ruffians were gathering.

"Is that who I think it is, William?" Dr. Root pointed to a man dressed in a fine suit. "He certainly looks like a politician."

"Yes, that is Senator David Rice Atchison," William answered. "He's a staunch proslave man. He rode in earlier this morning."

"Of course," Joseph answered thoughtfully. "The notorious single day President."

"What does that mean?" a fellow prisoner asked.

William shook his head back and forth in disgust. "In 1849, Atchison was President pro tempore of the U.S. Senate. On inauguration day, newly elected President Zachary Taylor and Vice-President Millard Fillmore, refused to take the oath of office on a Sunday, so some of Atchison's supporters claim he was president for the day since he was supposedly next in the line of power."

David Atchison was a forbidding presence even from that distance. He had dark shiny hair, deep set piercing eyes, and a nose and mouth that demanded attention. His entire being was fused with arrogance.

Surrounding Atchison and Stringfellow were more Border Ruffians than William had seen since they'd arrived in the territory.

William, Joseph, and the other prisoners were ushered behind a large tent where they could hear Senator Atchison's speech. As the morning wore thin, so did William's ability to hold his temper. The Senator brazenly bragged about the very same atrocities that filled William with rage.

"Men of the South and of Missouri, I am proud of this day," Atchison boasted. The outdoor arena erupted in rowdy and boisterous applause.

"Ruffian brothers," he continued as his audience hollered and shouted in praise, "I have served in the greatest republic the light of God's sun ever shown upon, but that glory, that honor was nothing compared with the solid grandeur and magnificent glory of this momentous occasion."

William looked over at his friend, Dr. Root. Their eyes connected, angry sparks flying between them, hotter with every word the Senator spoke.

"I stand here," Atchison continued, "on this beautiful prairie bluff, with naught but the canopy of heaven for my covering, with my splendid Arabian charger for my shield, whose fleetness I may yet have to depend upon for my life. Unless, with this day's work, we shall drive from our Western world those infernal emigrants and paupers, whose bellies are filled with beggar's food, and whose houses are stored with Beecher's Bibles."

Though Atchison was said to be one of the finest orators of his generation, William and his companions could not believe the effect this man had on his audience. Every word he uttered brought them to a more fevered frenzy and Atchison was not finished yet. He pointed to the red flag held by one of his men.

The flag flapped over his head in the morning breeze.

"Pleasing beyond my powers of description is the fact that above me is the only flag we recognize, and the only one under whose folds we will march into Lawrence. This flag is the one under which these prisoners were arrested, who are now outside yonder tent endeavoring to hear me, which I care not if they do! Yes, this puritan stock will learn their fate, and they may go home and tell their cowardly friends what I say! This large red flag denotes our purpose to press the matter even to blood. The lone white star in the center denotes the purity of our purpose, and the words Southern Rights above it, clearly indicate the righteousness of our principals! Now hasten to your work and follow Colonel Stringfellow to a glorious victory. We will assist you in crushing the last sign of abolitionism in the territory of Kansas!"

When he finished speaking, the prisoners watched as Atchison rode to the edge of town. The crazed and drunken crowd followed him, yelling and pumping their weapons against the sky. Stringfellow turned his horse around and trotted over to his group of prisoners.

"My men are anxious to join the fight and since I have no one to stand guard, you are all free to go." Stringfellow glanced down at the scene beginning to unfold on the streets of Lawrence. "We ride now to join Senator Atchison, Sheriff Jones, and his posse. I suggest you leave if you value your lives and thank your lucky stars you have the opportunity to do so." He turned his horse around, looked at the smoky horizon and let out a belly laugh. "I must hurry! It seems the festivities have already begun and I don't want to miss the party." He then joined the ranks of the hundreds of Border Ruffians descending into the town.

"Come on," William hollered at his companions. "I have no idea if we can do anything to help, but I must see what's happening."

William, Dr. Root, and several of the others who'd been imprisoned, ran across the ridge to the highest point. William froze, his unbelieving eyes silently witnessing the destruction of the city. They had a clear view of the main streets of Lawrence.

"We have no weapons or horses! What can we do? We're absolutely useless to them." William fell to his knees as he

watched people scatter from their houses and businesses as they were rushed by the enemy. Women and children clung to each other in terror.

"There is nothing we can do, William," Joseph said, feeling as helpless as his friend. "Oh, no! Over there, William." He pointed to a frantic mother chasing her little boy into the street. "He's running straight for that cannon." The woman caught and pulled him back as the two men pushing the cannon laughed at her horror stricken movements. She held on tight as she carried the boy toward the river, not looking back for fear they were being followed. But the ruffians had better things to do.

William saw Stringfellow catch up to Atchison in the street. Sheriff Jones and his posse were surrounded by hundreds of men darting in and out of buildings all along the route.

When they reached the Free State Hotel, Stringfellow and Atchison were greeted gleefully by the cheering, shouting crowd already gathered there. Atchison dismounted and joined the two men with the cannon. They stood guard on either side of the weapon, just outside the front doors of the beautiful Free State Hotel. Atchison bent down and lit the fuse dangling from the canon. He covered his ears as a loud noise, accompanied by a belching trail of smoke, whistled through the air. The round of ammunition shot over the hotel, landing in the fields on the other side.

Laughing and slapping each other on the back because of the gross error in their aim, the cannon was reloaded. The drunken celebratory atmosphere filled William and Joseph with rage. They watched at least fifty more rounds of cannonballs hit their mark, but the strong stone walls of the brand new hotel still stood. The men loading the cannon were not pleased.

"What are they doing now?" Joseph watched as Stringfellow and a second group of men entered a building across the street. A minute later, several of the ruffians exited the *Herald of Freedom* newspaper office carrying boxes of typeset and other printing equipment. Joseph knew that since they started printing it, the *Herald of Freedom* had become the most important antislavery media in the territory. These men apparently knew it also, and were jubilant as they carried the profits of their looting down the street. William could see through the front windows of the building as the press was smashed to bits with axes and sledge hammers. Some others began throwing newsprint and various supplies out the windows of the second story. The wind caught them, spread them across the rooftops, and out into the prairie beyond the town.

"They are going to throw the typeset in the river!" William's eyes followed the men until they arrived at the muddy banks of the Kansas River. The boxes made a huge splash as they were hoisted and heaved forward. Other printing equipment followed the boxes of typeset into the river and sank out of sight.

"What a waste," cried Joseph. "Now Stringfellow and his men are piling books in the street! There must have been an entire library in there!" Dr. Root watched horrified as one man set the book he was holding on fire.

"They mean to burn them!" Dr. Root put a hand to his head as the torn pages caught and passed the flame through the huge pile of books, creating a blazing bonfire.

William looked down the hill where they were standing. The spectacle continued to unfold before them. Several women and children were struggling up the slope, trying desperately to find the safest place they could reach.

"Take cover!" William shouted as he watched an incendiary missile shoot from the cannon. A blast from the depths of the hotel caused the women to drop to the ground on top of their children. William ran down the hill to assist them as the walls of the hotel finally exploded and fire consumed the building. "Come on. Just climb a little higher and you'll be safe."

"Hurry, men. They need help." Joseph tore his eyes away from the burning books and hotel and led several of the former prisoners down the hill to assist William with the ladies and children attempting to climb up.

"Here, let me see that leg." William looked at one boy's bleeding thigh, waving for Dr. Root to come take a look.

"Thank you," his mother said. "At first I thought it was just a scratch, but it's still bleeding." She stepped back as Dr. Root lifted the boy in his arms and carried him further up the hill. His mother's gaze shifted to William.

"Thank you for your assistance. I ... I didn't know what to do." She broke down crying as they reached the top of the hill, and William helped her sit on the grass beside her son. The little boy lifted his arms and wrapped them around his mother as some other women and children joined them. Dr. Root kneeled beside them and tore a strip from his own shirt to bandage the bleeding leg.

"We told our husbands we would wait here for them." Tears streaked the woman's dirty face as she saw the walls of the once beautiful Free State Hotel crumble to the ground amid a cloud of smoke and dust.

Sheriff Jones, Atchison, and Stringfellow were apparently through. William and Joseph watched the trio ride toward the outskirts of Lawrence. Their men apparently had orders to cause as much wreckage as possible before they exited the town. They began pillaging and setting fire to anything they didn't want to carry away.

The refugees stayed on the hill for another hour or so observing silently. They were too numb to move. Finally the raiders, who had successfully sacked their once growing and prosperous town, departed Lawrence and rode east.

William rose, waved his hat, and cheered when the outlaws were chased by a valiant band of men intent on filling the ruffians backsides with bullets. It was a useless effort by the Lawrence defenders, but William understood and respected their determination to drive out the last of the proslave forces.

Soon after, the women and children started to wander down the hill as they spotted husbands and fathers looking for them. Some walked back into town alone to see what was left of their homes and families.

Dr. Root walked over to William as the last of the women reached the bottom of the hill. "I overheard one of the men say he saw John Brown and his men stop some of the ruffians from destroying more houses. Stringfellow and Atchison had already left town by the time Brown's reinforcements arrived," he said. "They heard about the attack and came to help. Only they were too late. As they left town, he heard Brown swear that the slave-owners and their thugs will pay for this day."

William's fists clenched and his eyes blazed blue fire. "I have never felt so helpless and useless in my life!" He expelled a breath and quietly added, "Unfortunately, I believe this could be only the beginning of a real war."

William and the others walked back across the ridge as the afternoon sun began to sink. They returned to the camp to see what they could find of their missing belongings. They hoped to regain possession of the stolen letters, but they could find nothing left except a bowie knife and one of their mules.

"This old boy looks like he didn't fare any better than we did in this prison. He probably hasn't eaten or had much water all week. We could try to take turns riding him on the way home," Joseph said, "but I'm not sure this poor old mule will even be able to carry us one at a time."

"Let's at least go back through Lecompton on our way home," said William. "Maybe someone in the territorial capital can do something about our being imprisoned and the theft of the letters. However, we shall most likely never see our weapons or the other mule."

The local militia captain said there was nothing more he could do. "I truly sympathize with your plight, sirs. If you would allow me, I would like to personally pay you back for your revolver," he said. William accepted his offer.

With nothing more to be done, the two friends headed home.

"I was afraid those roughnecks were going to shoot us this morning. I was certainly glad they decided to allow us to leave instead," Joseph said to his companion.

"Well, the only options they had were to kill us, leave us locked up to break out on our own, or let us go," William replied. "To be honest, I am surprised they chose to release us but grateful to God they did so. Even with losing the letters, our guns, and our other mule, it is good to be returning to our new home.

CHAPTER 8

The Prairie Guards Join the Fight

Wabaunsee, Kansas, May 22, 1856

William and Dr. Root arrived in their rough new hamlet the next day before nightfall. They encountered no further trouble on their journey home.

"You men have had quite an experience," Charles Lines said after William finished telling him about their ordeal. "A messenger from Topeka was here yesterday. He informed us that Governor Shannon will be resigning his position forthwith and returning to his home in St. Louis."

"Perhaps what happened truly did have an impact on him," William said. "I believe he wanted no part in taking sides in the battles that are sure to come."

"I can see that more fighting is still of great concern," Charles said. "Fortunately, in your absence we began to organize a military unit. We even took a vote and elected our new leader."

"I'm happy to hear it. That will save time and allow us to be ready to offer our assistance that much sooner," William said. "Have you given thought to a name for the group?"

Charles grinned and extended his hand. "Congratulations, Captain Mitchell. You are the man we elected to lead the Wabaunsee Prairie Guards."

A few days later, the newly formed military unit held their first parade to formally welcome back their commander, Captain William Mitchell. The parade music was provided by "Coe's Band." It consisted of Mr. Coe himself as leader and only member, beating time upon a tin milk can. The company marched to Bisbey's Spring where "the band" served cold water to the men using his "instrument" to fill their cups. The orderly sergeant assisted using another tin pan.

The company then marched around William and Joseph, "imprisoning" them in a square. They all sat down to listen to a few special speakers, including Dr. Root. Joseph told the men about their time of imprisonment in Stringfellow's camp and William's near death experience. He also gave his eyewitness account of David Atchison's speech and the subsequent sacking of Lawrence. When he was finished, the sergeant stepped to the center of the square. He unrolled a piece of paper and began to read the list of resolutions that had been drawn up when they elected Captain Mitchell. As the last one was read, William bowed his head.

"Be it resolved that we welcome Captain Mitchell to the command of this Company, conferred during his absence, and express our pleasure at coming under the authority of one whose wisdom and courage inspire universal confidence."

After Charles prayed and said a few more words, William stood and addressed the handful of ragtag troops.

"Men, I am very proud and humbled to have been elected the new Captain of the Prairie Guards. A commander is only as successful as his troops. I believe you will all stand beside me, strong and brave, as we wage this war against slavery until victory is achieved. We have pledged to fight alongside our Kansas brothers who have already summoned us to come to their aid."

The men listened intently to his every word. "Be prepared to be away for several weeks," William continued, "as we don't know how long our support will be needed. We will leave for Lawrence as soon as possible. Stand with me now. We will close this meeting and be on our way. The battle has already begun and we must join it straightway."

Captain Mitchell saluted his men and they returned the gesture. Then he addressed two young men standing close to him who held their Sharps rifles at the ready by their sides. William had to hide the smile that tickled the corners of his mouth at their youthful eagerness to contribute a formal firearm salute to end the festivities.

"Attention!" William faced the duo. They took aim, raised their rifles to the sky, and held the pose awaiting their Captain's command.

"FIRE!"

The two soldiers pulled the triggers at the exact same moment, the loud reports echoing across the neighboring fields. At the last echo, Captain Mitchell called the first official gathering of the Wabaunsee Prairie Guards to a close.

"Company, dismissed!"

PART THREE

Henrietta's Story:
Maude's Wooden Box

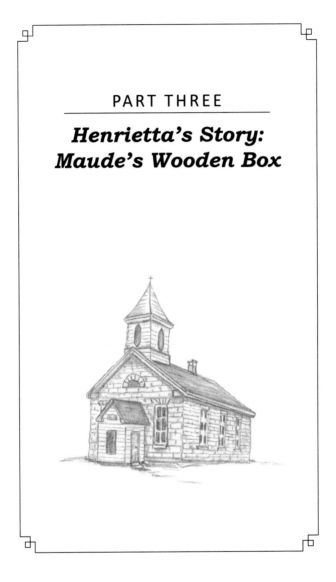

CHAPTER 9

Letters to Connecticut

August 26, 1932

Maude added a final stroke of blue to the sky above the church. "There, girls," she said as she put the brush down and wiped her hands on her smock. "I think it's time to get some lunch and let this masterpiece dry a bit."

"But Maude, you can't stop your story now! You never told us about the wagon yet!" Irma Jean jumped up and grabbed Maude's smock like she was going to forcibly detain her if necessary. "I mean I liked hearing about your daddy almost gettin' hanged and all but what about the wagon and the slaves?"

Maude ruffled Irma Jean's hair. "I tell you what. Why don't you girls go home for lunch and ask your mother if you can ride over to my place this afternoon? I have some things in my cedar chest I want to show you before I tell you the rest of the story."

"Come on, Henrietta!" Irma Jean pulled on her boots, then yanked me to my feet. "Last one home's a rotten egg!"

"Thanks, Maude," I said. "We'll see you in a little bit." Irma Jean was already mounted up on Trixie and headed down the lane. "Mama probably does have lunch ready for us and is wondering where we are by now. But I'm sure she won't mind if we come over later."

I waved at Maude from atop my horse, then followed Irma Jean home, just far enough behind to let the dust settle.

◇◇◇◇◇

Maude was sitting on the porch in a rocking chair when we arrived at her place after lunch. She held a wooden box in her lap. Irma Jean and I tied our horses up and joined her.

"What you got there?" Irma Jean ran her hand over the top of the box before sitting down on the bench beside Maude's rocker.

"That's what I wanted to show you," Maude said. "Henrietta, you can have the other rocking chair. That one belonged to my Aunt Agnes. This one was my father's."

Maude opened the box and pulled out some old yellow newspaper clippings.

"Charles Lines didn't go fight with the Prairie Guards that summer because he was needed in Wabaunsee to oversee the building process. He planned to return to New England to raise funds for the church and school but until he could get there, he found a way to keep family and friends in Connecticut aware of the company's progress in Kansas. Charles wrote these letters and they were published in the *New Haven Daily Palladium* and other Eastern newspapers."

Maude handed the clippings to me.

"My Aunt Agnes saved them. Henrietta, would you like to read them to us?"

I took the fragile paper from her hands and began to read.

June 11, 1856

It has come to our attention that false reports of our well being and the general state of things here in the Kansas Territory have been circulated there in New Haven. We were very disturbed to hear that one news source even reported that while imprisoned in an enemy camp recently, William Mitchell and Dr. Root were shot and killed. To set the record straight, both Mr. Mitchell and Dr. Root have returned from their captivity and are in good health. We will do our best to keep such false reports from causing any further grief and despair to family and friends by sending regular accounts to be posted in this newspaper.

I am now in Lawrence, with several others of our company, on our way to Kansas City for the purpose of hauling up our steam engine and sawmill. I am writing to you in full view of the ruins of the Free State Hotel, whose destruction was witnessed by Mr. Mitchell and Dr. Root. After conversing with citizens here in reference to the plundering of private houses, it is hard to believe that we live in the country for whose liberty Washington and his compatriots fought, and martyrs among them bled and died. The only comfort in the case must be found in resorting to the foundation of our faith, where we find the assurance that God can cause the wrath of man to praise him.

—*Charles B. Lines*

"The next letter," Maude said when I'd finished, "is what Charles wrote in preparation for his fund-raising visit, so the people would know why he was coming and be prepared to give."

I carefully gave the first clipping back to Maude and unfolded the second piece of newsprint.

June 17, 1856

It is not surprising, perhaps, that a community of 2,000 people should grow up so rapidly. But it is lamentable to witness all through Kansas how little is being done to establish the worship and the ordinances of our holy religion. We hope our own community will not be so tardy in the matter, but after the example of our fathers, make it the first business to provide a good house for the worship of God, and another for the education of our children."

"Wasn't that an intelligent way to communicate with family and friends back in New England? Having the newspaper print the letters saved Charles from writing more than once." Maude folded the newspaper clippings and slipped them back into the bottom of the box. Then she took out several envelopes. They too, looked old and worn.

"My father also kept his family informed but not through the newspaper. These are some of his personal letters. This first one is to my grandfather."

August, 29th, 1856
Lawrence, Kansas

Dear Father,

We have heard reports indicating efforts to raise funds on our behalf are well underway. We are most anxious to begin construction on a church and school.

The Prairie Guards are again in war with the Border Ruffians. It appears as if they intend to give us no rest until this question is settled. We received another message from Lawrence on Saturday calling on us to come to their assistance again. We arrived there Thursday evening and found the town filled with people, I would say around six hundred armed free-state men. The Free State Hotel, which Dr. Root and I witnessed the destruction of in May, has been converted into a fortification.

We have already been engaged in several battles. We number around forty and have good quarters here and hope this thing will be settled soon.

Please do not feel uneasy on my account, as I will take care of myself. Remember me to those inquiring.

Your Affectionate Son,
William A. Mitchell

"This letter was written while he was still in Lawrence fighting with the Prairie Guards." Maude continued reading.

September 30, 1856

Dear Father,

We are still stationed in Lawrence under the command of James Lane. A few weeks ago, we began an assault on a proslavery settlement at Hickory Point. I was in charge of the cavalry, and we were armed with our Sharps rifles.

Lane sent a messenger carrying a white flag of truce. Two or three came out to meet him, there was a short conversation and then our messenger returned to the Commander.

He informed Lane that the leader of the gang told him to 'take this dirty paper back to your leader and tell him we will fight him and all the hireling cutthroats and assassins he can bring against us.' The battle ensued.

The next day, Lane received orders from Governor Geary to disband his troops and he departed for Nebraska on other business. The Prairie Guards returned to Fort Lane for the Sabbath.

Since the battle of Hickory Point, it has been an exciting time as John Brown has again arrived on the scene. We heard that he and his men were present on the

day of the sacking of Lawrence and pro-
claimed that justice for the deed would be
done. Many a proslave man has felt his
wrath since. I am sure you have heard of
his notorious national efforts in the cause
of freedom.

Recently, Brown and his men were
traveling through Kansas with a wagon-
load of slaves, when they were intercept-
ed by a party of proslavery men. They
called for his surrender, but Brown paid
no attention and continued his march.
Both sides were well armed, but John
Brown and his followers were ready and
willing to die for their cause. Their op-
ponents were not. His would-be captors
cowered away, leaving Brown to continue his journey.

I had the occasion to fight beside John
Brown soon after. He met up with the
Prairie Guards and proceeded to give orders with all the "coolness of a farmer going about his evening chores," as one of
my men put it.

The enemy line was formed at the sum-
mit of a ridge, awaiting orders to attack.
They fired a few shots and then nearly
all of them dropped back under the shel-

ter of the ridge. John Brown gave word to move forward, which we did. Upon attaining the ridge we discovered our foes in full retreat. Whether they were unaware of our actual numbers, which were far less than theirs', or they had caught sight of old John Brown and decided not to engage us further, we shall never know. With a parting salute of gunfire, we marched back to Lawrence.

Please remember me to everyone there.

Your Son,
William

Irma Jean rocked back and forth on the bench. All of a sudden she jumped up and yelled. "John Brown was there when they sacked Lawrence, right?"

"Very good, Irma Jean," Maude praised her. "I'm glad you were paying attention to that part of the story." Maude opened another envelope.

"A year later, in the summer of 1857, my father was preparing for my grandfather and Aunt Agnes to come to Kansas. Charles Lines was back in New England by then and they were going to be traveling back to Wabaunsee with him and several others. My father wrote this to Aunt Agnes before they left."

June 13, 1857
Wabaunsee, Kansas

Dear Agnes,

I am anxious for you and Father to come to Wabaunsee with Charles Lines and his family. I know the other men are anxious to see their wives, children and sweethearts who will be coming with you. It has been a long hard winter and we are glad to feel the warm Kansas sun on our backs.

We have built a temporary wooden structure to serve as our church until construction can begin on the stone church for which Charles has been raising funds. We have the building site picked out and are looking forward to getting started. Plans for a permanent schoolhouse and a hotel are underway also.

Our own cabin is completed and will be ready when you arrive. My prayers will be with you as you travel across this great land. Give my love to all.

Your affectionate brother,
William

Maude replaced those letters in the box and took out one last envelope. She pulled out the letter.

"During the next two years," she said, "my father and some of the other neighbors around here were very active in the Underground Railroad system. Do you know what that is, Irma Jean?"

"Is this the part about the slaves and the wagon?" Irma Jean stood up.

"It's almost time for that," Maude answered. "This letter was to my Aunt Jean."

October 7, 1858

Dearest Sister Jean,

The leaves are beginning to turn here in Kansas. We should have beautiful autumn color this year. The cottonwoods are the first to show their bright yellow, but the hardwoods which line the Kaw, our name for the Kansas River, will soon be blazing with red and orange.

Agnes is busy with her garden, preserving what she can for the winter. She was a great help with Father, but is keeping busy with other things while he is there visiting with you. She has been of great help to me.

We are in the process of gathering materials to build the stone church. It will probably take several years to complete but we are anxious to begin. Perhaps construction can start by next summer. In the meantime we are happy to have our temporary meeting place and an official charter. Agnes is teaching Sunday School.

My job with the Railroad keeps me busy. In fact, my letter writing was just interrupted with a message from a fellow conductor informing me that I have some cargo that needs to be picked up tonight. It is for shipment on the next train and appears to be an unexpected package that will require some careful handling. I had better close this correspondence and be about my duties.

With love and affection,
Your brother, William

"The people who worked on the Underground Railroad couldn't talk about what they were really doing. It would be too dangerous for everyone. You will see why in a minute." Maude turned to Irma Jean. "Sit down now and I will tell you about the slaves and the wagon." Maude put the last letter away and set the box on the bench.

"My Aunt Agnes told me this story many times when I was your age. It was my favorite. It was a sad and scary story but also full of hope and love."

Irma Jean backed up and I lifted her into my lap. I adjusted her legs over mine and gave her a little hug. "We're ready, Maude," I said.

Irma Jean snuggled into my arms. Maude cleared her throat.

"Tell us everything," my little sister whispered.

PART FOUR

Maude's Story: The Underground Railroad

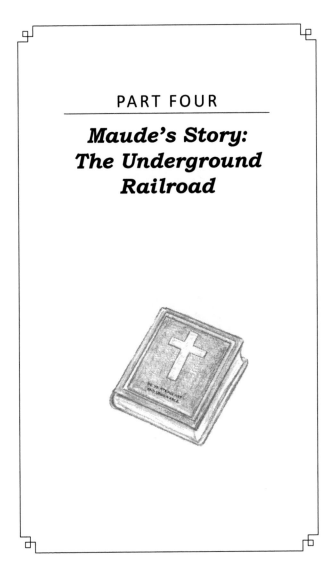

CHAPTER 10

Safe at the Station House

Wabaunsee, Kansas, October 8, 1858

William swung his lantern back and forth three times. His "package" should be waiting for him behind the stone wall. A brother and sister the message had said. Their mother hadn't made it. He didn't know when they had been dropped off, but they had probably been hiding there since early morning. William pulled his wagon up beside the stone wall and jumped down to the ground.

"Is anybody there?" William stood silent waiting for an answer.

A muted whisper drifted across the ditch. "That's him, Abby. Come on."

William could barely make out their silhouettes crouched under the tree until the young teenage boy stood up and helped the little girl to her feet. The boy ducked under a low hanging branch and stepped toward William, but the girl hesitated. William could see the whites of her eyes shining with fear as she stared at him. Trusting a white man would come hard for her he knew.

The boy's shirt and the girl's dress, which probably used to be light colored, were tattered and hung loose and limp on their thin frames. They were now dingy with dirt and streaked with dried mud, but it helped them blend in with the darkness of the night, which under the circumstances was a good thing.

"I'm scared, Jesse." Abby cowered behind her big brother, her face peering around at his elbow.

"Stay behind me," Jesse instructed as they moved forward.

William wondered how these two children had made it this far alone. Jesse was clearly the older and very protective brother, but still so young to have such responsibility thrust on his slender shoulders. He wondered what had happened to their mother and if her children had witnessed whatever it was. Even in the dark, William could see the bond between these two siblings and his heart went out to both of them.

"I'm sorry it took me so long," William whispered. "My name is Captain William Mitchell. You will be staying with me and my sister for a few days."

William walked to the back of the wagon and looked down the dirt road in both directions. "It's all clear—come on over here. Quickly now."

Jesse and Abby obeyed, scrambling over the stacked stones onto the deserted lane. Though they both wore shoes, William could see that they were worn and had several holes and didn't fit properly. At least they were able to lend their feet some measure of protection from the elements. That was more than many of his charges had when they came to him.

Captain Mitchell reached for the pitchfork stowed behind the wagon seat. The children watched as he moved the mass of prickly yellow prairie hay. It smelled good—fresh and earthy.

"It's gonna be itchy," Abby complained in a whisper to Jesse.

"No, it won't be," Captain Mitchell said smiling at the little girl, trying to put her at ease. "See, I put a blanket down on top and doubled it over. If you crawl in between the layers of blanket, you'll be nice and comfortable even when I put more hay on top."

"See, he's made it real nice," Jesse said to Abby, playfully pulling on her shiny black braids. Unused to some white people being nice to her, especially men, she hung her head and looked down at her shoes, the customary attitude for a slave girl when in the presence of the master.

"Hurry up, now, little one," the Captain said, his heart wrenching at the sight of Abby's submissive stance. He wondered how badly she had been treated in her young life.

Jesse helped Abby up into the wagon, holding the blanket open for her. When she was settled, he jumped up and crawled in beside her. After covering them with more hay so they were out of sight, Captain Mitchell climbed into the wagon seat.

Extinguishing the lantern, he guided the hay wagon down the road by the natural light of the moon. Normally, they wouldn't transport passengers on the line when the moon was almost full, but these two children showed up when none of the agents were expecting them. They were supposed to go with their mother on another route north, but when they were separated, the children were sent west to Wabaunsee instead. Captain Mitchell was the closest conductor with a station house that could accommodate them for a few days. He didn't like the fact that they had to hide all day before he had gotten the message that they were here, but sometimes that's the way it had to be.

"I think we're safe, but keep still until we get there," the Captain said. "It's not far now, just down this road a short distance. Agnes will have something prepared for you to eat. After that you can get some sleep."

The children were very quiet. Captain Mitchell wondered if they had fallen asleep. He turned into another lane, and looked back when he heard one of them moving around. The boy peeked out from the under the blanket just in time to see the Mitchell cabin come into view. As the wagon rolled to a stop, Captain Mitchell jumped down and walked around to the rear. He lifted the hay again, and Jesse jumped to the ground.

The door of the cabin opened, and William's sister stepped out onto the porch. She was a tall woman with a strong frame. She wore a white apron over a light colored dress—it looked light blue in the moonlight.

She was holding a book in the crook of her arm. When she saw William gently lift Abby to the ground, she flashed a smile in the little girl's direction that warmed the night air instantly. Her strawberry blonde hair was laced with silver and

drawn up into a bun, although several stray strands danced about her head in the evening breeze as she briskly walked to the back of the wagon.

"Oh, you poor wee dears," she exclaimed in her native Scottish brogue as her smile faded to pure concern. "Come here. We'll have you fixed up in no time. My name's Agnes, the Captain's elder sister." Agnes gently put an arm around Abby's shoulders as she led the children back to the porch.

William knew there was no woman better than his sainted sister to ease the pain in the girl's heart. Agnes had never married and had children of her own. She had taken care of their mother until she passed away and had brought their father to Kansas to continue caring for him. Agnes was eight when the family left Scotland, so between that and living with their parents all her life, her Scottish accent was still evident.

William watched Abby look up at Agnes. Twin tears rolled down Abby's cheeks, tracking down her dusty face. He figured Abby was thinking about losing her mama. William was fairly certain the children's mother either remained a slave or that she was dead. He was grateful to have Agnes here to help him with his "passengers," especially the young ones who had seen such tragedy. She had a knack of making them feel safe and loved.

Abby still clung to Jesse's hand, but the corners of William's mouth turned up as he noticed Abby gently ease her hand out of Jesse's and take the one Agnes offered as she guided them inside the house.

"And who would you be, now?" Agnes asked.

"I'm Jesse, Ma'am," said the boy as he looked around the cozy cabin. "And this here's my sister, Abby." A hesitant smile appeared on Abby's face. Agnes cherished it knowing there had probably been few smiles lately.

"Welcome, child," Agnes said. "Make yourself at home, Abby dear. You, too, Jesse. I have ye supper all ready."

Before William left to pick up the children, he told Agnes the message from the previous conductor had said they were forced to leave their mother behind.

"Oh, William," she'd said, "I can't imagine how difficult all this must be for them, especially the wee one. A girl needs her mama."

William and Agnes both smiled as they watched Jesse's eyes grow wide. The boy looked over at the curtain-drawn window where a wooden table held two china plates and two blue glasses filled to the brim with milk.

"Something smells like Christmas in the big house in Missouri," he told Agnes. The aroma drifted from the old iron stove standing beside a tin-door pie-safe and an icebox.

"Ah, 'tis a surprise for ye," Agnes said with a wink in Abby's direction.

William interrupted, remembering the seriousness of their situation. "I don't believe you are in any danger of being tracked tonight, but it's best to keep you out of sight as much as possible," he said. "I see Agnes has chicken legs, cornbread, and glasses of milk waiting for you." He nodded at his sister. "Agnes is an excellent cook. After you're done eating, I'll show you where you'll be staying for the next day or two."

It was apparent that Jesse and Abby hadn't eaten a real meal in several weeks. They sat on wooden stools and attacked their chicken and cornbread while they watched Agnes and the Captain.

Captain Mitchell moved the sideboard a couple feet away from the wall. Walking behind it, he reached up and pulled down a stack of small rose-patterned plates, which sat on the top of the built-in china shelf. The shelves were a foot deep, two-feet wide, and ranged six to ten inches apart, spanning the area from the top of the sideboard almost to the ceiling. The top two shelves held small plates, the next two, matching cups and saucers, and on the bottom two sat dinner plates which completed the set. Agnes reached up and took each stack from the Captain, placing every one on the sideboard as her brother gently removed them from the shelves.

"Be careful now, William," Agnes warned. "Those are grandmother's dishes, don't ya know. Don't be a dropping and breaking any of them again."

Captain Mitchell paused for a moment to look at Jesse. "Jesse, sisters never let you forget anything. I dropped one of these cups when I was but a boy. We lived in Connecticut at the time. Agnes made sure our mother knew I was the culprit." Captain Mitchell smiled at Jesse then turned back to Agnes. "However, my dear sister, during your move to join me here in Kansas, I believe several items were broken on the journey, so I am not the only unfortunate one to accidentally destroy our family treasures. I rest my case." He laughed as Agnes pursed her lips and shook her finger at him.

"Never you mind that," Agnes retorted. "Ye jest be careful now." Turning to Jesse and Abby, she noted that their food and drink were gone. "Well, that musta tasted good! Now for me surprise, I have molasses cookies in the oven. They should be out soon."

"Cookies?" Abby spoke for the first time. "The folks at the big house ate those. They really for us?"

"Well, not all of them," William said, "I claim a few for myself." He stepped back from the now empty china rack and reached over to get a pole propped up in the corner. "This is my fishing pole, but it has other uses, too."

William put the end of the pole against the ceiling right at the edge of the wall and gave it a little push. A section of the ceiling lifted completely out and the Captain skillfully edged it to one side of the opening. The trap door was completely hidden by the seams of the ceiling boards. Jesse would never have known it was there until it moved.

"Now, dears, up ye go, like this." Agnes hefted her skirt up a bit and raised her foot in the air. "Well, give me a boost, William." The Captain gave his sister a foot-up and supported her while she got her footing on the bottom shelf. She grabbed the top shelf with her fingers. Then she slowly climbed up each shelf until she could pull herself into the hole in the ceiling. Agnes lit the lantern while the Captain helped Abby climb up. Jessie went last. After they were all safely up, William climbed on a chair and stuck his head through the opening.

The loft was small, barely more than a crawl space, not more than eight feet long, and five feet wide. There were no windows, but a foot-square door was set in the center of the stone part of one wall, an extension of a chimney from the room below. A chamber pot sat beneath the small door. A couple blankets and pillows lay on the cot sitting against the far wall. A basket, tied to a rope, sat beside the open hole in the floor.

"Right there's a vent in the ceiling, mind ya, so you have fresh air, but it won't rain in, don't ya worry," Agnes assured them. "That door in the stone wall is part of an old chimney. At the bottom is a very deep hole so you can open the door and empty the chamber pot in there and it won't bother a soul."

Agnes pulled out her hankie and dabbed her nose. "Twice a day, one of us will knock on the ceiling with the fishin' pole. When ya hear the taps, you'll know 'tis safe to open it up. Lower the basket down on the rope and I'll fill it up with something for ye to eat and drink."

William added, "We never know when someone will show up unannounced, looking for runaways. So, you have to stay up here most of the time and keep quiet."

Agnes looked apologetic for the conditions Jesse and Abby would have to endure, but she needn't have worried. Jesse assured her their little attic loft was nicer than the place they'd lived with their mama.

"And this is a hundred times better than places we've had to hide since we crossed the river two weeks ago," Jesse said. "We never had a place that was this warm and dry. Especially with food and drink twice a day."

"Oh William, I forgot about my cookies! Get them out for me, please. I'll be right down." William ducked out of the hole, jumped down, and headed to the wood-burning oven. Agnes slowly backed down the hidden ladder and landed below with a thump. A few minutes later she called up at Jesse to lower the basket. After Agnes put something in it, he pulled it back up, and he and Abby both reached in the basket. At the same time, the two runaways took a bite of the best thing either of them had ever eaten. Abby swallowed, the delicious wonder causing her mouth to break into a smile at the pure sweetness within. She leaned forward.

"Captain? Mizz Agnes?" Abby peered down through the opening. "Them's the best thing I ever did eat. Mama said always be grateful. Thank you for takin' good care of us since Mama can't. You must be angels."

Agnes removed her handkerchief from her pocket again. The sound of her sniffling was covered by the scrape of the trap door sliding shut.

CHAPTER 11

The Young Refugees

The Mitchell Homestead, October 10, 1858

While Jesse and Abby stayed in the Mitchell's loft, they slept a lot and ate everything that Agnes sent up in the little basket.

"It sure is nice to have a full stomach, Mizz Agnes," Jesse told her.

After dark on the second night they were there, the Mitchells let Jesse and Abby come down to the living room so they could visit awhile. Agnes knew they must get bored having to stay up there alone so much, but it still wasn't safe to transport them further.

"Do you know any Bible stories Mizz Agnes?" Since Agnes taught Sunday School, she was delighted to hear Abby ask. "Would you like me to quote some scripture verses Mama taught us?" Abby stood up straight.

"Mama's mistress used to read to her from the Bible every night," Abby told Agnes.

Jesse added, "And Mama listened to them stories and memorized as many verses as she could."

"And she taught them to us!" Abby's grin sparkled in the lantern light. "My favorite verse is the one where the Apostle Paul said, *"And my God shall supply all your needs according to His riches in glory."*

"I like the story about how the Israelites were slaves in Egypt, and Moses led them out to the Promised Land," Jesse said. "We're gonna find our promised land, too. I know it."

Jesse and Abby both got quiet. William could tell they were thinking about their mother.

"Jesse, what happened the day you had to leave your mother? Can you talk about it?" Agnes was concerned for both the children, but Abby's little face broke her heart.

"I pray for her every night," Abby whispered. "I say, 'Lord, keep Mama safe and please supply her needs like you is supplyin' ours.' Then I thanks him for you baking us them cookies."

Abby yawned and crawled up in Agnes' lap. "You can tell them about Mama, Jesse. Maybe Captain Mitchell can help find her."

"We left our shack in Missouri," Jesse began, "Mama, Abby, me, and Emma. Emma was Mastuh's daughter, but she was always our friend. She couldn't bear it when her daddy told her he was selling Abby."

"Emma was like my big sister," Abby said. "I miss her, too."

"Our neighbors worked on the Railroad—just like you, Captain. Emma asked them to help and he arranged for us to all three be picked up the night before Abby was to be sold." Jesse leaned back and thought a minute.

"Somehow Emma's daddy found out we were gone. I don't think he knew Emma helped us—least I hope not." Jesse paused to look at Abby. She had her eyes closed. "We were supposed to be picked up at the river, but just as the raft came into view, we heard the wagon. It was Emma's daddy. He jumped down when the wagon came to a halt and aimed his rifle at me. I tried to shield Abby and Mama best I could." Jesse hung his head.

"He told us to hold it right there or he'd shoot me. 'Fore I could do anything, Mama pulled Abby and me back toward the river. She put herself between us and his gun. Mama yelled at him that she'd go back if he'd let us go." Jesse paused and took a deep breath.

"He told her there was no way that was gonna happen and to step aside. See, Emma's daddy bought and paid for our whole family. He told Mama that she'd pay for trying to escape, just like our daddy did."

Jesse put his head in his hands and William reached over and put his arm around his young shoulders. He felt Jesse stiffen before he went on.

"He made us watch as Daddy got beat. The next day Daddy was sold. We haven't seen him since." Jesse swiped a hand across his eyes.

"Jesse, I am so sorry," William said softly. "At least you and Abby got away from that man."

"Mama pleaded with him to let us go," Jesse continued, "but he wouldn't give in. I saw Mama grab the barrel of the rifle and pull it sideways. She leaned into him and knocked him to the ground. Then Mama yelled at me to take Abby and git on the raft."

Agnes hugged Abby gently.

"I had to fight Abby all the way but I carried her splashing through the waist-deep water to the raft." Jesse's voice broke. "She screamed at me not to go without Mama."

"There was nothing else you could do," William said. "If you hadn't been brave enough to get Abby out of there, all three of you would have been caught."

"There were some other runaways who helped haul us both onto the raft.

When I looked back, Mama was on the ground. He dragged her to the wagon, lifted her up, and practically threw her onto it. The last thing I saw was Mama raising herself up and looking at us. I barely heard her voice across the water. She said to keep Abby safe and that she loved us both."

William sighed and Agnes soaked up another tear from her cheek with her hankie.

"Before we ever set out that night," Jesse told William, "I promised Mama I'd take care of Abby if we got separated. I have to keep that promise."

Abby stirred on Agnes' lap. She opened her eyes and unconsciously twirled her braid around her finger while Jesse went on.

"The man that picked us up after we got off the raft took us to a barn where we hid in the loft for several days. Then another man picked us up, dropped us off at the stone wall, and told us to stay out of sight till you picked us up that night. That's how we got here."

"Aye, an' that's enough storytelling fer tonight," Agnes said lifting Abby off her lap. "Ya both get on up to the attic now and try to get some sleep."

William put a hand on Jesse's arm. "Things are going to be much better from now on, son. I guarantee it."

Jesse nodded, then helped his little sister up the hidden ladder to their safe hiding place, and peaceful sleep.

◇◇◇◇◇

Jesse and Abby stayed with the Mitchells several weeks. There had been strangers in the area asking questions about runaways, although no one seemed to be looking for two children on their own. Still, William didn't feel that it was safe to move the children yet, and besides Agnes felt it was giving them time to heal from having to leave their mother.

One night in early November, Jesse and Abby had finished their supper and were already asleep. William was sure he'd already roused them by making a ruckus in the kitchen. He "tapped" the fishing pole on the trap door. Except for the night when Agnes talked William into letting the children come down for awhile, the china dishes and sideboard had not been disturbed. There was always the possibility of unwanted visitors, and it took a while to use the china shelf as a ladder.

William slid the sideboard across the floor, the legs scraping against the wood planks. The clink of the dishes being stacked on top of it made Agnes wince. Hopefully, the hurried commotion wouldn't result in breaking her grandmother's china. When William used the fishing pole to move the loose piece of ceiling, both children's faces appeared in the opening.

"More company has arrived, Jesse," Captain Mitchell said softly. "Try and make room for them. I hope you won't have to stay up there together for long. I know it will be cramped."

Abby and Jesse inched backward as a black head of hair sprinkled with white, popped through the floor. In the flicker of the lantern's flame, two rows of white teeth and a pair of smiling eyes reflected back at them. The man climbed out and then another person came, and another, and another. Captain Mitchell appeared last. He was tall enough that his whole head and shoulders went through the trap door opening with him standing flat-footed on the sideboard. He looked at the six more runaway slaves crowded into the little attic loft.

Jesse spoke first. "My name's Jesse. This here's my sister, Abby. We been here three weeks now, right Captain?"

William looked around the crowded room. "That's right, Jesse." Turning to the older man he continued. "These two children came across the river from Missouri a while ago. I will let you introduce yourselves."

"Well, son," the man with the bright smile began, "we're from Texas and we been on the line now for two months. Glad to meet you." The older man reached out his hand to shake Jesse's. Abby stood behind her brother and didn't say a word.

"My name's Zeke" he continued, "and this here's my wife, Gertie, my sister, May, and my three children." He pushed a boy about Jesse's age forward. "This is Ben, and over there is Lizey. The little one we still call Baby Jane even though she's almost four."

"I'm sorry the accommodations are not larger, but you should be safe here for now," William said. He watched as everybody sat down wherever they could find room. It was crowded with eight bodies in the tiny room, but William supposed they had dealt with cramped living quarters before.

"I'd like nothing better than to see the wide open spaces that freedom will bring, but for now it is good to have my family safe," Zeke said. He and Gertie sat on the floor. Exhausted from the day, Baby Jane was sound asleep in her daddy's lap. Jesse shared the mat with Abby and Lizey.

Ben sat on the floor in front of his Aunt May who settled on the cot. William winked at Jesse when he caught him stealing a second glance at Zeke's daughter, who looked a few years older than Abby.

"Agnes will send up some supper directly. Then try and get some sleep. I'll make arrangements for further transport in the morning," William said. Suddenly he ducked down to look in the kitchen.

"William! I hear horses," Agnes whispered loud enough for everyone to hear.

William jumped down off the sideboard and hissed up at the hole in the ceiling, "Get that trap door shut and don't say another word until I give the all clear. Somebody's coming up the road!"

The attic dwellers heard Agnes and the Captain quickly set the dishes on the shelves and shove the sideboard back against the wall. William glanced up as Jesse dropped the trap door in place. Captain Mitchell's sharp eyes scanned the room. They heard footsteps on the porch and then a knock. William nodded at Agnes, then walked over and opened the door.

"Good evening, gentlemen. What can I do for you?" William greeted the men as Agnes stepped forward and blocked the doorway as much as she could. She wasn't about to let anybody in the house this late at night.

"We're tracking a passel of runaway slaves—a whole family of them. They were spotted up in these parts earlier today, but they got away from my boys over by the creek in Wabaunsee." The older of the two men standing on the porch peered around Agnes, trying to see into the room. "We were a half mile up the road when we noticed someone carrying a lantern from the barn to the house. Did you see anyone?" The two men looked at each other with devilish sneers. "Even in the dark, you can see the whites of them runaway's eyes you know!" Both of the men let out a hateful laugh.

Captain Mitchell didn't move a muscle. Neither did Agnes. "No, sir, we have seen no light tonight but the bright stars and moon God put in the heavens. Now if you'll excuse us, my sister and I were about to retire."

Without waiting for a reply, the Captain shut the door, bolted it, and Agnes blew out the lantern on the table. They heard some muttered words on the other side of the door as their visitors left the porch. William peeked out the window and watched in silence until they mounted their horses and rode away. Agnes let out a sigh of relief as the two riders finally disappeared over the hill.

"We best try and get those poor folks across the river as soon as possible, William," she said. "I know we've had a cold snap and tonight's not going to be any warmer, but I don' see how they can all stay up there together much longer. Can ya get them out tonight or is it too dangerous?"

"I think we should wait until tomorrow. I need to contact the Smiths to help. Eight is too many people to manage on my own." Captain Mitchell put his arm around Agnes. "You better prepare a late dinner for Zeke and his family and send it up. They've had a long night and they probably haven't eaten in a while."

Agnes relit the lantern and busied herself in the kitchen as the Captain tapped on the ceiling with his pole. "They're gone for tonight," he told Jesse when he stuck his head through the hole, "but you'll all have to stay here for another day. Lower that basket and Agnes will send up some supper for our new visitors in a minute. Then I hope you will be able to sleep, for tomorrow we may be traveling all through the night."

CHAPTER 12

Hidden in the Big Wagon

Road to the Kaw River, November 13, 1858

Agnes was going to save the last of the batch of molasses cookies, but she decided her guests could use a treat, so she sent up a few. She wished there were enough cookies for each of them, but they could share. She put the food into the basket for Jesse to hoist it up.

"Jesse, if ye an' Abby save a cookie 'til the others eat their supper, everyone can have a half before a goin' off t' bed." Agnes gazed up through the open trap door while William stood guard at the front door. They continued to visit with their guests while they ate. But William kept glancing out the window to make sure those men didn't return.

"Mizz Agnes, thanks for them good vittles," Zeke called down to her after supper. William heard him rise to his feet. A thump on the ceiling was accompanied by an "Ouch!" William cringed knowing Zeke was having trouble dealing with the small space. He looked up at the hole in the ceiling as Zeke spoke again. "Well, I s'pose we may as well try and figure out how to stretch out best we can and get some sleep now." Zeke bent over and looked down into the kitchen. "Night, Captain, Mizz Agnes. That sho' was a fine supper."

Agnes and William listened from below as Zeke helped his children find room on the floor. He asked Jesse if May and Gertie could share the cot. Abby had enjoyed sleeping on it since they arrived, so she agreed to lie on the floor with the rest of the children. Zeke leaned up against the wall right by the trap door, the only other space available. "Don't forget to say your prayers now and thank the good Lord for getting us this far safe and sound."

Echoes of "Thank you, Jesus," were the last words William and Agnes heard before Zeke slid the trap door shut.

◇◇◇◇◇

Captain Mitchell was up at dawn and Agnes listened to him ride off toward their neighbor's house. Joshua Smith lived just up the road from William. He had once escaped hanging by the border ruffians just like William. Joshua was released because being from England, his accent and prematurely gray hair caused them to think he wasn't part of the fight.

Joshua brought his family and settled in Wabaunsee the year before William arrived. John Smith, his eldest son, worked with his father on the Underground Railroad. Joshua was a station master and hid slaves at his house. John lived in a little cabin on the river, too small to hide slaves, so he became a conductor and helped transport them north to the next station.

William knew he'd need a bigger wagon to accommodate the eight people hiding in his attic. They had to travel several miles to the ford where they would be able to cross the Kaw River.

Enoch Platt, another conductor and neighbor, would meet William at the river. Enoch came to Wabaunsee a year or so after William. He was from Illinois where his family was also involved in the Underground Railroad. Enoch was returning from a journey guiding the most recent group of runaways north. Usually he made the runs from the other side of the river alone. This time Captain Mitchell would go with him to the next station which was located close to the Nebraska line. The Underground Railroad went all the way to Iowa, Chicago, and Canada. There, the slaves could start a new life.

Captain Mitchell's only concern now was getting his wards to the banks of the river and across without them being seen. He wished he knew where those two scoundrels were who stopped by the house last night.

"Morning, Joshua, John." William greeted them. Joshua and John Smith were already out doing chores when the Captain pulled up his horse.

Morning, Captain," Joshua replied in his gruff voice. Joshua Smith looked every bit an Englishman—rugged but regal even in his homesteader's clothing. His hair and beard were wiry and mostly silver. John Smith favored his mother more, but was a handsome man with dark hair and beard.

"I'm going to need some help this evening if you don't mind," William told them. They never talked openly about the arrangements for transporting slaves, even if they were alone. You never knew who might be hiding close by. The Captain felt the need to be especially careful with those two men searching the area for the refugees. "Let's go at the usual time. Bring the big wagon and your team of oxen."

The Smiths agreed and Captain Mitchell headed back to his cabin to make further preparations.

William found Agnes busy packing a bucket with food. She included cornbread, apples, cheese, and a few pieces of cured bacon. Carefully rationed, this should last the party of eight until they reached the next station house. Thinking of little Abby, Agnes reached in the cookie jar and pulled out the last four molasses cookies. She wrapped them up in cloth and placed them at the top of the bucket. She smiled thinking of the look on the little girl's face when they were unwrapped for tomorrow night's supper.

Captain Mitchell stood on the porch of his cabin and watched the sun slowly sink below the horizon, leaving the deep blue sky streaked with varied hues of orange and pink. He loved Kansas sunsets where nothing blocked the view of God's masterpiece painted across the heavens. He continued to watch as the first stars appeared, but then his brow crinkled with concern as he noticed a bank of clouds gathering. They looked like snow clouds. William felt the heavy threat of early winter weather in the air. He shivered.

It was almost time for the Smiths to arrive. So far the weather held, but by the time they were ready to leave, there were no stars visible in the cloudy night sky. After the former slaves vacated their attic hideaway and wrapped in as many warm clothes as Agnes could find for them all, John Smith helped them lie down side by side on their bellies across the width of the wagon. The littlest one needed to be on the outside because she would be easier to hide in the hay.

"Jesse, you best hold on tight to me out here on the edge of this wagon," Abby said. "I may be the littlest, 'cept for Baby Jane who has to stay by her Mama. But I don't wanna get bumped off!"

"I got you, Abby, don't worry. And Ben's holdin' on to me, and Lizey's holdin' on to him, and May has Lizey, and Gertie's got May, and Zeke's got Gertie, and Baby Jane! So none of us is goin' nowhere but straight to the river!"

"Don't worry, Abby," Captain Mitchell assured her. "I will be sitting on the back of the wagon to watch the road behind us. You won't fall off."

"Hopefully, in the middle of the night we'll have the road to ourselves," Joshua told them. Joshua didn't usually go along, but this way John didn't have to come back alone, and it would be nice to have an extra set of eyes this trip.

Agnes watched the loading of the wagon. The yellow and brown rag rugs she'd made blended in well. They were laid out flat on top of the hay. Once everyone was in place, she walked over to Abby and pressed a black book into her small hand. William watched his sister. This little one was special to her. He knew it would be difficult for her to say good-bye.

"Take this, Abby girl. I want ye to have it. Maybe someday you will learn to read, and this book's the best reading in the world." She leaned over and kissed Abby's cheek.

"Thanks, Mizz Agnes. I'll keep it forever, and I will learn to read. I promise."

Agnes bowed her head and offered a prayer for safe travel for the party.

"Lord above, bless all these, your children, and wee Abby especially. She misses her mama so much, so if you could take care of her too, that'd be a blessing. In Christ's Holy Name, Amen." Abby squeezed her hand and then Agnes stepped back.

Captain Mitchell and the Smiths covered them with the second rug and then started pitching more hay on top.

When they finished covering their cargo of travelers, the former slaves couldn't be seen at all. They'd take it slow and easy so as not to arouse any attention. Thankfully it hadn't rained the past few days and the roads weren't too rutted.

Joshua and John climbed into the wagon seat and Captain Mitchell settled himself in the middle of the back of the wagon. The spoke wheels turned in response to the pair of oxen pulling the rig from behind the cabin where they'd been hidden for loading. They slowly made their way down to the Old Military Road. William sat on the back of the wagon, Abby snuggled up against his back, unseen. Agnes waved at them from the front porch. William saw her dab her eyes with her handkerchief as she closed the door of the cabin.

The company traveled through the night arriving on the banks of the Kaw River at daybreak. In the first light of dawn, Captain Mitchell could see that nobody was on the other side of the river.

"Where is Enoch do you suppose?" William and Joshua shared a concerned look.

"Boy, it sure feels good to get up and stretch out," said Zeke as he unfolded his long legs. He stood up, crawled over the seat, and jumped to the ground. He was the only one too tall to lay flat in the wagon. He'd had to lie on his side with his knees bent back under the wagon seat. His generous feet were covered up with a blanket. "The rest of you stretch a little, but stay put 'till we see what we're up against. Now, what can I do to help, Captain?"

Joshua and John were already down at the water's edge poking around with a piece of driftwood. Joshua looked back at Captain Mitchell.

"The shallow edge of the water's completely iced over to about eight feet out where the current is running. There's enough movement out there to keep the middle of the river flowing, but to get across we'll have to chop a section of ice out here on the edge as wide as the wagon," he said.

Zeke and John looked for pieces of wood big enough to do the job while Joshua began to stab at the far end of the ice with the pitchfork. Captain Mitchell made sure the women and children were safely secured sitting in the middle of the bed of straw. He climbed up on the driver's seat to wait for the other men to clear a path for them to cross.

The river was shallow right there, but out in the middle the water still rose axle deep on the wagon wheels. Unfortunately, close to the banks of the river, the shallow depth also allowed the water to freeze over faster.

"Easy, boys, we almost have it." John had done this before so he gave instructions to his father and Zeke. "Here's what we're gonna do," John said. "Once this cake of ice under us breaks free, we three will pole ourselves out into the open water. When we make it across and hit the ice on the other bank, we'll have to jump off this piece of ice and let it go on. Then we'll cut out another slab of ice the same size on the other side, so the wagon can get through. Understand?"

Zeke and Joshua steadied themselves. The moment their ice raft was cut loose, they would help push it into the middle of the frigid water. None of them wanted to lose their balance. In that current, it wouldn't take long to carry one of them down the river. Given the water temperature, a man could freeze and die of exposure in moments.

John took a last stab and the chunk of ice broke free. The three men worked together to get themselves out into the current and across without drifting too far downstream. When they hit the ice on the other side, they jumped over one at a time, each reaching out and pulling the next man to safety. They stood on the other side and watched as the slab of ice they'd used as a raft, broke apart on some rocks just a few yards down river.

"That was close." John and Joshua looked at each other but set about their next task without further comment. It wasn't long before the second piece of ice was cut and shoved out to join its companion on the rocks.

With a clear path cut on both sides of the river, Captain Mitchell urged the team of oxen forward. Twenty minutes later they were hoisting themselves up the other bank with the wagon in tow. Just as the back wheels cleared the water, Enoch Platt appeared at the top of the rise. He waved a greeting and headed down the hill.

CHAPTER 13

The Blizzard

The Road North, November 14, 1858

Joshua and John Smith were ready to head home as soon as they helped transfer the party of eight and their supplies to Enoch's wagon.

"Thanks, men," Captain Mitchell said to them. "Enoch and I will finish this leg of the journey with Jesse, Abby and Zeke's family. Take care on the way home. Remember those two men will be looking for all of us."

He hopped on the wagon seat beside the driver. "Let's go, Enoch. Root's Trail awaits."

"You mean Lane's Trail?" Enoch smiled. William's friend, Dr. Joseph Root was the one who laid out the trail north to Nebraska back in the summer of 1856. But it was named after Commander Jim Lane. The Prairie Guards served in Lane's regiment that same year, fighting against the Border Ruffians. "You always give credit where credit is due, William. Dr. Root would appreciate it, I'm sure. By the way, I'm glad to have company on the trip back home."

"My pleasure, Enoch," Captain Mitchell said with a grin, "but I figure your gladness is because Agnes will invite you to supper when we return to the cabin."

"True," Enoch answered. "I shall never pass up a chance to join the Mitchells for a meal."

Captain Mitchell turned his attention to the people in the wagon. He was especially fond of Jesse and Abby, and he wanted to make sure they had clear passage north. William wished he could find out what happened to the children's mother. It would take a miracle for them to be reunited with her, but his God was in that business. William had ceased to be surprised at miracles a long time ago.

After the cold night, the sunshine took the bite out of the air and they made good headway.

"This is a more deserted part of the line so it requires no night travel, or making anyone hide under a haystack," William told his passengers. "Let's enjoy the day."

They all got better acquainted as they covered the miles. Enoch Platt's double team of horses made much better time than Joshua Smith's pair of oxen.

Still, William kept a wary eye out for the two men who had landed on his doorstep looking for Zeke's family. Jesse noticed him scanning the horizon.

"Captain, what would happen if you and Enoch were caught helping us?" Jesse wondered if Captain Mitchell and others like him were risking their lives to do this.

"Remember those two men who were looking for you? We have to very careful of people like that. If they caught us red-handed helping slaves to freedom, we could be shot. They consider it a crime. The Underground Railroad is as dangerous for the conductors and station masters as it is for the slaves who use it."

"Thank you," Zeke said. He'd seen Captain Mitchell searching the skyline for danger. He figured he was making sure they weren't being followed, even if this was a safer passageway. "We owe our lives to you and all the brave men who got us this far. We woulda never made it alone."

William and Enoch exchanged a knowing glance. It was the right thing to do and they'd decided they would continue to transport slaves to freedom as long as they could.

As the day drew to a close the sun disappeared behind a dark bank of clouds.

"I thought maybe we'd outrun this storm, Enoch. I was afraid it would catch up with us last night, but we managed to stay ahead of it. However, I believe we will see snow tonight."

They made a brief stop to rest and divided the supper Agnes had packed. Abby and Baby Jane squealed with delight when they found the cookies. They were still tasty, but Abby was so cold all she could think about was how good they were that first night when they were at the Mitchell's cabin, fresh and warm out of the oven. It wasn't long after she swallowed the last bite, that she felt a snowflake fall on her nose.

"Jesse, it's startin' to snow."

"I see it. Just stay close. I'll keep you warm."

Those first few flakes soon dissolved into sheets of blowing snow and ice. The temperature dropped rapidly and it got so thick in so short a time that Enoch and the Captain were unable to find shelter before they were blinded by the storm. The company huddled together under the blankets, and the drivers kept the wagon moving while they searched through the blizzard for any sign of a stand of trees where they could take cover from the elements.

"It must be midnight, William," Enoch yelled over the wind. "I'm afraid we're hopelessly lost. I know the way by heart, but in the storm I couldn't see any of the landmarks I usually use as guides."

"Over there!" Captain Mitchell shouted. "In that ravine. It looks like some trees. Check it out."

Enoch urged the horses toward the blurry shadows Captain Mitchell had spotted. Sure enough it was a small wooded area with a frozen stream. Jesse and Abby jumped out of the wagon followed by Zeke and his family. They stood under the tree branches until William and Enoch were able to get a fire started.

"Thankfully, I always carry flint and steel," Enoch told them as he pulled out a box from under the wagon seat. "And here's dry wood wrapped in this piece of oilcloth. I've experienced the ever-changing Kansas weather before, so I try to be prepared for anything. As the saying goes, if you don't like the weather in Kansas, just wait ten minutes!"

Once the wagon was empty, Enoch's team pulled it forward, and found shelter under a nearby tree. Frozen horse-breath snorting from their nostrils surrounded the animals like a cloud. By huddling together close to the fire all through the long night, the horses and their passengers kept from freezing to death in the sudden Kansas blizzard.

"Too bad we don't have a real underground railroad," Enoch said. "It would be a lot warmer."

The storm passed as quickly as it came. At dawn, Enoch climbed a small hill not too far away, to get his bearings.

To his great surprise, the very house they were heading for stood only a short distance away.

The ten travelers immediately piled into the wagon, anxious for real shelter. The horses plowed through the field of newly fallen snow until they crested the hill. There the smooth round ruts of the trail were clearly visible under their blanket of white. They led directly to their destination. Enoch paused before descending, to view the sunrise.

"Lord, you surely do know how to paint a sky." Zeke said. Captain Mitchell liked the way Zeke prayed to God like he was right there beside him.

Upon arriving at the next station house, Captain Mitchell and Enoch Platt greeted their fellow conductor. They introduced his new charges starting with Zeke's family and then Jesse.

"And this little lady is Abby," Captain Mitchell said with misty eyes. He caught a tear with his thumb as it slid down Abby's cheek. She hesitated for a moment because she'd probably never come close to feeling this way before, but the next instant she threw her arms around the Captain.

"I never hugged a white man before," Abby stammered.

Captain Mitchell knelt in the snow and held her, neither saying another word.

The next wagon wouldn't be leaving again until nightfall but the Captain and Enoch needed to begin their journey home. After farewells were given, Captain Mitchell left the children on the porch and climbed up into the wagon seat beside Enoch. He turned to wave. Jesse had one arm in the air waving back and the other around Abby. She was clutching the book Agnes gave her.

"Thank you, Captain," they said in unison.

Jesse added, "Take care and God bless."

As the wagon started to move, Abby called out, "Wait!" Leaving Jesse's side she picked her way through the drifts of snow surrounding the cabin as fast as she could. Reaching up to grab the Captain's hand, her tears came again.

"I'm gonna miss you, Captain! Tell Mizz Agnes I loves her, too. And 'specially I loves her cookies!"

William laughed. "We'll miss you too, little one. Now go on back to your brother and you both get inside where it's warm."

Abby turned around and placing her small feet in the footprints she'd just created, she made her way back to Jesse. Captain Mitchell waved one last time as the wagon slowly moved forward, retracing its tracks over the snowy ground.

PART FIVE

Henrietta's Story: History Comes Alive on Old Settlers' Day

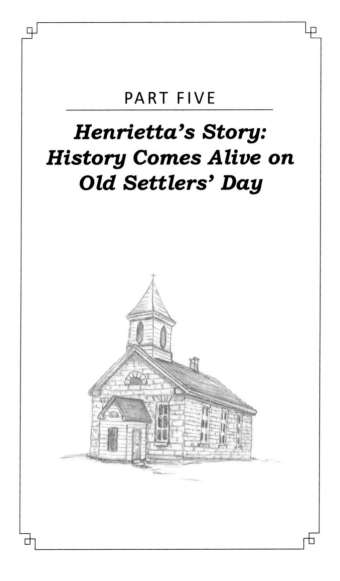

CHAPTER 14

Maude's Tale Ends and More Trouble Begins

Wabaunsee, Kansas, August 26-27, 1932

"And that, girls, is how the wagon in my painting was used to help the slaves escape on the Underground Railroad."

Maude finished her story and we both clapped. I hated to see the story end. So did Irma Jean.

"That was a great story, Maude." Irma Jean said. Then she scrunched up her forehead. "But what happened to Jesse and Abby?"

"I don't know," Maude answered. "I wish I did. Aunt Agnes only told me that part of the story so she must not have known what happened to them either."

"Do you think they really never ate cookies before Agnes gave 'em one?"

My little sister loved cookies as much as Abby apparently had.

"That is probably right," Maude said. "Slaves often lived in terrible conditions. There were some good masters who were fair to their slaves and treated them well enough, but many slaves had to go through some pretty tough times.

I imagine few slave children ever had anything as special as a molasses cookie to eat."

Maude paused a moment, like she wanted to make sure Irma Jean understood what she was saying. "They probably didn't sleep in a nice soft bed either. If they did anything wrong, it wasn't just a trip to the woodshed with a daddy who loved them and just wanted them to act right. Slaves were beaten with whips. That's why so many slaves were afraid to run away. The Underground Railroad made it easier for them to find freedom, but even if they managed to get away, they always had to be looking over their shoulder in case their masters were hunting them." Maude looked at me. "So, did you learn anything new, Henrietta?"

I was surprised how Maude's story held my interest—especially since it was history, which usually bored me. "I liked the part about Jesse and Abby best. Is that china shelf still in your house?"

"It sure is," Maude answered. "Come on in and see."

We followed Maude into the cabin.

"Here it is," she said pointing to the rows of dishes perched on the shelves. "Now there are steps beside it leading to the attic," Maude explained. "When we added on to the original log cabin, we made the second story bigger and turned the loft into my painting studio."

"Did you ever meet any slaves, Maude?"

"No, Irma Jean, I didn't meet any of them myself," Maude said. "I wasn't born until 1875. The Civil War was over by then and President Lincoln had already set the slaves free. But I heard that story from Aunt Agnes so much that I feel like I really knew Jesse and Abby."

"Thanks for telling us your stories, Maude. I really did learn a lot," I said.

"Well, girls, I enjoyed our afternoon," said Maude, "but I'm sure your mother will be looking for you soon. It's almost supper time."

We walked back outside and over to our horses. Irma Jean hefted herself up across Trixie's back and slung her leg over till she was sitting up as tall and straight as a six-year-old can get. I loosened the reins and handed them to Irma Jean.

"Now don't go racing off, you hear me? You wait ..."

But Irma Jean was already turning Trixie around, interrupting my instructions with her farewell. "Bye, Maude! See you tomorrow. Mama and Myra are coming with us to help get ready for Old Settler's Day on Sunday. They can see your paintin' in the morning." She dug in her heels and was gone in a cloud of dust.

"That girl." I mounted my own horse, waved at Maude and followed the cloud—just far enough behind so I wouldn't have to eat dust for supper.

◇◇◇◇◇

Maude was at the church when we arrived the next morning. As my sisters and Mama climbed out of our buggy, Irma Jean planted her feet where they landed. I hopped down beside her.

"We can't go in yet, Mama," Irma Jean said. "You and Myra have to see Maude's painting first!" She grabbed Myra's hand and tugged. Mama and I followed them over to where Maude was sitting in front of her easel in the side yard of the church.

"Good. It's dry enough," Maude said, gently touching the canvas. "Hello, Lena. Good to see you, Myra. I have a surprise for Irma Jean and Henrietta, so I'm glad you are both here, too. I put the finishing touches on this last night so it would be ready to be framed and displayed for Old Settlers' Day tomorrow."

"Hey!" Irma Jean started dancing around the easel like a jumping bean. "Look, Mama, right there! It's Maude in front of her easel, and me and Henrietta sitting on the ground watching her paint the church! We're in Maude's painting!" Irma Jean continued to ride her invisible Pogo stick while Mama, Myra, and I admired Maude's artwork.

Sure enough, Maude put all three of us right into the painting. "Wait a minute," I said. "Irma Jean, come here and look closer. We're not the only ones in the picture. Look up in the tree."

Maude laughed and stood up beside me. "That didn't take you very long, Henrietta."

Irma Jean stopped leaping about and studied the painting, feet apart and fists on her hips.

"There they are!" She pointed and resumed her hopping. "I see 'em, too." She turned and looked at me. "It's Jesse and Abby sitting behind those branches. They're eatin' cookies and waving at us!"

"That's wonderful, Maude," Mother said clasping her hands together under her chin. "I love how you make your paintings so personal. You girls are very blessed to be in one of Maude's paintings. You better tell her thank you."

Irma Jean threw her arms around Maude's middle. "Thank you, thank you, thank you! I love bein' in your painting."

"Me, too, Maude," I added. "It's nice having such a talented artist as our neighbor."

"Now," Mama said, "we better go inside and see what we can do to help."

"Do we hafta?" Irma Jean whined.

Mama cast a stern look in her direction. She said no more.

Mama, Myra, and Irma Jean entered the church, but I stopped in the shadow of the doorway. I'd heard a car come chugging around the bend. Aunt Jo pulled up on the other side of the horses and buggy and shut off the engine. Her shiny black shoes hit the ground with a force that propelled her body out of the vehicle like her limbs were spring loaded. She slammed the door. I could tell by the expression on her face that she'd seen us. Maude knew it, too.

"She's here, isn't she?" Aunt Jo squared her shoulders and marched past Maude, without a glance at her painting.

"Josephine, hold on for just a minute. Friend, for your own sake you better be decent to Lena," Maude scolded. "This community is supposed to work together today to get ready for our big celebration. You best not cause any trouble and spoil it for everyone." Aunt Jo hesitated a moment but didn't say any more as she continued up the sidewalk. I ducked into the sanctuary of the church just as she stepped through the door. Maude followed her.

"Good morning, Jo," Mother said quietly as she and Myra stood in the aisle beside the front pew. "Say hello to your Aunt Jo, girls." Mama reached behind her back, extracting Irma Jean from amid the folds of her skirt.

"Hello, Aunt Jo. It's good to see you," my ever gentle sister Myra said as she walked over and gave our aunt a hug. I nodded and muttered a short greeting. Irma Jean merely stared, her eyebrows and mouth pinched together defiantly. She didn't know exactly why Aunt Jo didn't like her mama, but she knew it all the same. My little sister wasn't about to be nice to Aunt Jo if Aunt Jo wasn't going to be nice to Mama.

"Thank you all for coming, ladies," Maude said, disrupting the awkward moment. "Now let's see what still needs to be done."

We all received our assignments from the committee and set about the tasks at hand. Maude and Aunt Jo sat down at a table in the back of the church to finish preparing old photographs and memorabilia for the display. Mama and Myra were put in charge of polishing the pews downstairs and Irma Jean and I climbed the stairs to the balcony to dust the benches up there. We scrambled up the winding stairs.

While wiping down the front bench, I leaned over the railing. I could see Aunt Jo was staring at Mama, who was performing her cleaning task with the utmost care.

"Well," Aunt Jo said under her breath to Maude, but loud enough that I could hear her upstairs, "at least Lena is putting her expertise to work cleaning the pews."

"Jo!" I could tell Maude couldn't believe her words. She pulled Aunt Jo out into the vestibule and lowered her voice so nobody could overhear the conversation. But their voices drifted right up the curving stairway. I could hear them plainly in the balcony. Irma Jean was dancing her duster over the old straight-backed pew like it was a ballroom floor. I was glad she wasn't paying attention.

"You are no better than the slave traders with an attitude like that,"

Maude continued. "What makes you think you're so superior to Lena? Your money may make you more important to some people, but here in this church it's the condition of the heart that matters."

Maude walked back into the sanctuary. "Sorry, ladies, but I need to frame my painting. I think Jo and I have sorted through everything we want to include in the display." Maude glanced back at Jo. She was sitting at the table again, staring at the photographs laid out before her.

I continued to look down at Maude and Aunt Jo. Was that a tinge of shame on Aunt Jo's face? Maude saw it too because she looked up at me and smiled. Then she left. Perhaps Aunt Jo's heart was finally beginning to soften.

CHAPTER 15

A Surprise Visitor Joins the Celebration

The Old Stone Church, August 28, 1932

It was a glorious August morning. The sun was shining, and a cool breeze blew through the trees surrounding the old stone church. Tables were set up in the churchyard waiting to hold the delicious food the Willing Workers Society had prepared for Old Settlers' Day. My stomach growled as we slipped into our back pew and sat down.

"Good morning, Henry," Jo said. "Lena." Aunt Jo stood in the aisle with her hand stretched toward Mama and Daddy. "It's good to see you … both."

Daddy looked at Mama, then silently took Jo's hand. "Morning, Jo."

Mama stood up, leaned over, and gently kissed Aunt Jo's cheek. "It's going to be a wonderful day, don't you think, Jo? We have much to celebrate."

For the first time in my life, I saw Aunt Jo smile at my mama.

Daddy put his arm around Mama when she sat back down, a smile barely curving his lips. Aunt Jo walked to the front of the church and sat beside Maude.

The morning service proceeded as planned with several speakers sharing how seventy-five years ago their relatives started the First Church of Christ in Wabaunsee.

I was glad Maude had already told us her stories. It made it even more exciting to hear how others in the congregation were related to the Beecher Bible and Rifle Company or the original settlers who were already in Wabaunsee when the group from Connecticut arrived. Even Irma Jean sat quietly and listened to the speakers.

Mama and Daddy sat at the end of our pew. They were holding hands. Now that I knew how Aunt Jo gave them trouble when they got married, I was so proud of my parents. It was a lot like how my great-grandpa and Captain Mitchell stood up for the slaves and helped them start new lives. I was glad Aunt Jo had finally come around and wasn't mad at them anymore. I think Maude helped her see that what she was doing was as wrong as the way the slaves were treated.

Daddy always told me God made him and Mama for each other. After everything I'd learned the past couple days, I believed it now more than ever. My big sister Myra was sitting next to Mama. Next to Myra was her beau, Alfred. They were holding hands, too.

The song leader asked for anyone who'd ever sung in the church choir to come up and help lead the singing. About fifteen people went to the choir loft in front. Irma Jean poked me in the ribs with the hymnal.

"Find the page for me," she whispered.

I held the hymnal while the organ played the introduction to *Amazing Grace*. I started to sing but some movement in the back of the sanctuary distracted me.

As people joined in the singing, I turned toward Irma Jean, putting my arm on the back of the pew behind us. I saw a bent figure standing in the doorway behind me. Clutching a big straw bag with one hand and a cane with the other, the old woman looked around. She decided to sit in the chair resting against the vestibule wall which was usually reserved for an usher. Reaching into her bag, she pulled out a worn black Bible, opened it up, and laid it across her lap.

I knew I was staring, but I couldn't help it. I twisted my body more so I could see her without putting a crick in my neck. Irma Jean was so busy pretending she was reading every word of the song that she didn't notice my odd posture as I held the book.

The pump organ began to play another verse and the old woman sang along with everyone else. Under a straw hat that matched her bag, her salt and pepper hair curled around her face. The crinkled corners of her eyes blended into her wrinkled cheeks. Her lips parted to reveal a smile bright as the pearly gates.

Her gaze landed on me, then traveled down our family pew and back. I detected a tiny nod of her head before she turned her attention to the singing. Her deep rich voice joined in with the rest of the congregation. She didn't need a hymnal. She sung the words by heart.

"Through many dangers, toils and snares, I have already come;

'Tis grace hath brought me safe thus far, and grace will lead me home."

Listening to her sing almost made me cry. It was so … real.

The last notes from the pump organ faded away as the preacher stepped to the pulpit.

"Turn with me to John's Gospel, chapter 15, verses 12 and 13."

She found the verses quickly, like the book was an old friend she knew well. I got goose bumps as she ran her wrinkled hand across the yellowed page, tenderly stroking the printed words. As she reverently lifted the book closer to her face to read, I could see a faded name engraved on the front cover.

That's when I knew for sure. It was really her.

I couldn't pull my eyes away. She followed each line, tracing them with her fingers, her lips silently moving as the preacher read.

"This is my commandment, that ye love one another, as I have loved you. Greater love hath no man than this, that he lay down his life for his friends."

The sermon continued, but I was no longer listening. No one else seemed to realize she'd come. I liked being the only one who knew at that moment. My mind drifted to all the things I'd learned the past two days. Forty-eight hours ago I thought history was just a boring class in school. I dreaded it. But now I realized it was about real people and places. This church was real. She was real.

The preacher finally brought his message to a close. I had missed most of it, lost in my own thoughts. I knew his words were about the heritage of sharing God's love with the slaves and how our ancestors risked their lives to take them to freedom. But the sermon and all the other speakers and their stories didn't seem half as important as the story she could tell us.

A train blew its whistle in the distance. I love that sound. It's so mysterious and eerie, yet comforting and joyous at the same time. I had a feeling this day was going to turn out like that, too.

I wanted to stand up and tell the whole congregation she was here, but I couldn't make my legs or my voice work. I hated speaking in front of an audience worse than anything—just ask my teacher! But this was too important. I had to make myself do it. I stood up.

"Excuse me, Preacher, but I think we have a surprise visitor here today." All eyes turned to me, especially those of my parents. I couldn't believe I actually spoke out loud in church! But I couldn't keep this secret to myself any longer. "Maude, could you come back here for a minute. I think there's somebody's here you'll want to meet."

I slipped out of our pew and was the first to arrive at the woman's side. Maude was right behind me.

"Look, Maude. Do you know who this lady is?" I reached down and pointed to her now closed Bible. "See the name?"

Maude looked down at the Bible and then into the eyes of the stranger. "You have Aunt Agnes' Bible?"

I couldn't wait. I had to hear her say it. In a reverent whisper I asked, "Are you Abby?" She looked at me with that dazzling smile.

"Why yes, dear child, I am. How did you know?"

Irma Jean bolted out of the pew. She'd heard my question and then Abby's answer. Her jaw fell to her chest for a split second. The next instant she was yelling.

"Mama! Mama! It's Abby from Maude's story. It's Abby!" Mama touched a finger to Irma Jean's lips effectively silencing her for the moment.

Maude stared at Abby's face. All I heard was the wall clock ticking. Abby stood and the two women grasped each other's hands.

"Abby?" The old woman gave a trembling nod when Maude spoke her name. "Aunt Agnes told me all about

you and your brother Jesse and how you stayed in our cabin." Maude glanced in my direction then re-established her connection with Abby. "I just finished telling these girls the story. How in the world ..." Then the two women came together and held on like they were old friends long parted.

"Glory be to God." Abby's voice broke. "He brought me back to this place where I first felt real freedom." She took a deep breath, took a step back, and lifted a hand to Maude's cheek. "And to the family of my dear Mizz Agnes."

Irma Jean couldn't stand it any longer. "Abby, where'd you go after Captain Mitchell left you? That was the day after the blizzard, remember? Did your mama ever find you? What happened to Jesse? Is he gonna be here, too?" Irma Jean paused to look around for Jesse and to catch a much needed breath. "Did you go clear up north to Canada? What was it like bein' free? Tell us everything! Please, *PLEASE!*"

That outburst started a chain reaction of laughter that ran through the crowd like that train chugging down the tracks a few minutes ago. Most everyone there had heard Maude tell her stories before, so Abby was no stranger to most. There wasn't a single person who didn't want to hear her answer Irma Jean's questions.

"Let's go on outside and start our picnic," Maude suggested. "The tables are all set up under the trees. We can eat first and get acquainted." Maude paused. I think she was still trying to believe this was happening. "Abby, we want to hear where you've been the last seventy-five years." Maude grinned. "And then I have something to show you."

◇◇◇◇◇

Abby and Maude sat across from me while we ate lunch, sharing their history and a bowl of grapes.

"After your father left us," Abby began, "Jesse and I kept traveling with the family from Texas that we met in your attic. Zeke and his wife and children were such a blessing to us." Abby paused to pull a handkerchief from her pocket. "I was so lost without Mama those first few weeks. It took months before I could even talk about her much, except to Jesse. But Agnes, and then Gertie helped ease the pain of losing her. Zeke and Gertie took us in like we were their own."

"Where did you finally end up?" I asked.

"Zeke had planned to take his family to Canada. Jesse said we'd go wherever they went. After about a month of traveling the Railroad, we found a nice settlement of former slaves like us, in Minnesota. We decided to stay."

Maude leaned back in her chair. "Did you ever find your mother or get married?"

"No, Maude, we never found out if Mama ever escaped. That's the saddest part of slavery, how it broke families apart, never to find each other again," Abby answered with a trace of sadness. But her face lit up the next instant when a smile broke through. "But I know she'll be waiting for me in heaven."

"What about getting married?" I asked.

"I never married. Jesse married Zeke's girl, Lizey. I stayed with them and helped take care of their young'ns when they was small. They have four—two girls and two boys."

Abby looked directly at Maude. "Jesse and Lizey named their oldest girl, Glory, after Mama. The oldest boy is Zechariah, but they call him Zeke, like his grandpa." Abby took Maude's hand. "The other pair they named William and Agnes."

"Oh, Abby," Maude choked out. "Father would be so proud of that. Aunt

Agnes, too." This time Maude pulled a handkerchief from her pocket. "How is Jesse?"

"Oh, he and the family are doing fine. They has eleven grandchildren and one great-grandson. Jesse wanted to make this trip with me but he's getting' on up there. Why, he's almost ninety now, so he stays close to home. Lizey takes good care of him."

"So how did you know about Old Settlers' Day?" I couldn't believe Abby found out about our celebration today, let alone her making the trip alone.

"Well, Henrietta is it? Such a pretty name. My being here is a marvel of the good Lord for sure. We had a visitor back home last month. We found out he came through Wabaunsee on the Railroad a couple years after we did. The war was still on, but he escaped from South Carolina and came on up the line same as us. He remembered this town because of the Indian name and what it meant. 'Dawn of Day', he said, and it certainly was for all of us who came through here on the Railroad.

While we were swappin' stories, he mentioned that a friend of his from around here wrote and told him that you all was organizing a society to preserve the heritage of the church and the community. His friend even sent him a newspaper article from the *Wabaunsee Truth* telling about today. He showed it to me."

"An' you decided to come and surprise us, right?" Irma Jean had crawled up in my lap while Abby was telling her story. She'd been so quiet, I thought maybe she'd fallen asleep.

"Come here, chil', and give old Abby a hug." Irma Jean knew no strangers. I'm sure she probably felt like she'd known this lady all her life, so it didn't take her long to be swallowed up in Abby's arms. "Yes, baby," Abby continued, "I rode down with a family who were visiting folks in Topeka. I wanted to surprise everyone. But I'm the one who's had the nicest surprise of all, getting to meet all of you!"

Irma Jean popped off Abby's lap and ran over to Maude.

"Hey, Maude, what was the name of that preacher who sent Bibles and rifles here?"

"Reverend Beecher," Maude answered.

"Well, I think we should name our church the Beecher Bible and Rifle Church so folks would remember that name, too!" She leaned over and whispered something in Maude's ear, to which Maude nodded yes. Irma Jean disappeared inside the church.

"Well, my goodness" said Abby with a chuckle, "she certainly is a bundle of energy."

In a few seconds, Irma Jean appeared again, carrying Maude's painting. She had the canvas facing her so nobody could see the painting yet, but she held it away from her body because Maude had told us it takes a long time for oil paint to dry even if it seems to be dry on the surface. I was glad Irma Jean remembered.

When she stood in front of Abby again, Irma Jean set the bottom edge of her surprise on the table, standing up, but still facing away from Abby.

"This'll be the bestest surprise of all, Abby," Irma Jean told her. "While Maude was tellin' me and Henrietta the story about you and Jesse and Captain Mitchell, she was also painting ..." Irma Jean paused and turned the painting around. "... this!"

Abby inhaled as she placed her hand over her chest. She sat there in silence for a few moments just gazing at the painting, taking in the church, Maude sitting at her easel, and me and Irma

Jean on the ground. I saw her eyes slowly settle on the tree in the picture. As she recognized the images representing Jesse and her up in the tree, one glistening tear slid from the outside corner of her eye. I watched it spill into the channel of her wrinkled cheek and slide down her jaw before it dropped from her face, melting into the fabric of her dress. The spot where it landed turned from pink to burgundy.

"I was going to save this for my art show, Abby, but I want you to have it," Maude said.

"Oh, my goodness," Abby said. "This is the most beautiful painting I ever saw in my whole life."

I wiped my eyes. What a perfect day it had turned out to be.

"Abby!" Irma Jean handed the painting to Maude. "You gotta come with me now." She grabbed the fragile hand and led her new friend carefully across the yard. A table had just been filled with a dozen homemade desserts. My little sister turned to Abby with a twinkle in her young eyes that seemed to lock with the aged gleam streaming from the eyes of the former slave.

I knew exactly what Irma Jean was going to do next and she did it loud enough for all of Wabaunsee County to hear.

"Look at them all, Abby!" she cried spreading out her arms. "And you can have as many as you want. COOKIES!"

Discussion Questions

1. At the beginning of the story, Aunt Jo doesn't appear to like Henrietta and Irma Jean. Is there a similarity between Aunt Jo's attitude about the girls' parents and how masters treated slaves?

2. The Connecticut Kansas Company came to Kansas for two main reasons. What were they and why were they so important to them?

3. What part did Rev. Henry Ward Beecher play in their decision to come to Kansas?

4. The Company brought Bibles and rifles with them to Kansas. What was the purpose of bringing both?

5. Why did Maude think it was important to tell Henrietta and Irma Jean about the history of Wabaunsee?

6. What was the difference in the beliefs of the Border Ruffians and Free State men?

7. Why was the Wabaunsee Prairie Guards formed?

8. What war did the time they called "bleeding Kansas" lead up to?

9. John Brown was nationally known for wanting to abolish slavery. What do you think he did right? What do you think he did wrong?

10. The people of Wabaunsee who helped slaves escape on the Underground Railroad sometimes had to put their own families in danger. Would you have helped the slaves? Why or why not?

11. Which character in the story would you like to meet in person? Why?

12. The title of the book is *Dawn of Day*, which is the meaning of the Indian word Wabaunsee. Can you think of another title that could have been used?

13. Henrietta and Jesse both had younger sisters. How were their relationships as siblings alike? How were they different?

14. What is your favorite kind of cookie?

Activities

1. Take an UGRR tour.

2. Find the meaning of different Indian names. Choose a name for yourself or your class based on those meanings.

3. Plan your own classroom homecoming celebration with activities and cookies.

4. Choose your favorite scene in the book and have a drawing contest.

5. Write an alternate ending to *Dawn of Day*.

6. Learn about the new Mount Mitchell Heritage Prairie at:

   www.mountmitchellprairie.org

Selected Bibliography

Bird, Roy. *Civil War in Kansas*. Gretna: Pelican Publishing Company, 2004.

Connelley, William E. *A Standard History of Kansas and Kansans*. Chapter 27, Wilson Shannon, 1802-1877.

Cutler, William G. *History of the State of Kansas*. Chicago: A.T. Andreas, 1883. http://skyways.lib.ks.us/genweb/archives/a918/v1/ch27pl.html

Encyclopedia of Arkansas History and Culture. Isaac Charles Parker, 1838-1896. www.encyclopediaofarkansas.net

Goodrich, Thomas. *Black Flag: Guerrilla Warfare on the Western Border, 1861-1865*. Bloomington: Indiana University Press, 1995.

Goodrich, Thomas. *War to the Knife: Bleeding Kansas, 1854-1861*. Mechanicsburg: Stackpole Books, 1998.

Historic Lecompton: Political birthplace of the American Civil War, Capital City of Kansas Territory. www.lecomptonkansas.com

Kansas Historical Quarterly: Letters of Charles B. Lines. Kansas State Historical Society, Spring, 1956. www.kshs.org

Manhattan Mercury. September 14, 1986, February 2, 1997.

Manual of the First Church of Christ. Wabaunsee, KS.

Prentis, Noble L. *A History of Kansas.* Winfield: E.P.Greer, 1899

Rural Reflections: Portraits of the Past, Maude Mitchell. Sunflower Journeys, KTWU/Channel 11, 1998. http://ktwu.edu/journeys/scripts/1109a.html

Stubbs, Michael. *Brave Hearts and Strong Arms, the Story of the Connecticut/Kansas Colony.* Wabaunsee County Historical Society newsletter, 2006.

Territorial Kansas Online: Biographical Sketch, Benjamin F. Stringfellow, 1816-1891. http://www.territorialkansasonline.org

Topeka Capital Journal. August 21, 1966, April 6, 1969, December 27, 1987, May 17, 1995.

Wabaunsee County Historical Society. *New Branches from Old Trees: A New History of Wabaunsee County.* Author, 1976.

Wabaunsee County Truth. Vol. III, No. 2.

Wamego Smoke Signal. August 25, 1986, April 29, 1987.

Wamego Times. April 30, 1987.

About the Author

J.A. McPhail, (aka Jeanne Ann, aka Jeannie,) a native of the Sunflower State, possesses a rich fifth generation Kansas heritage. Her great-great-grandfather, John Willig, was a charter member of the Wabaunsee Beecher Bible Rifle Church, featured in *Dawn of Day*.

Born and raised in Topeka, Kansas, the author grew up attending many BBRC Old Settlers' Homecomings. As children, she and her brother sang a duet at one of the annual gatherings. Years later, after marrying her high school sweetheart and raising a daughter, the McPhails returned to the church several times, singing with the Messengers Quartet.

During the seven years as her full-time care giver, McPhail listened to her mother, Irma Jean, tell stories about her childhood growing up in the Wabaunsee area. History and family memories, combined with inheriting two Maude Mitchell paintings of her grandparents' homesteads, inspired the unique blend of fact and fiction used to create *Dawn of Day*.

As a former editor, columnist, and library director, McPhail has written hundreds of articles and columns for various newsletters, magazines, and newspapers. She currently writes devotions and maintains a reading/ writing page on her family's website, www. themacsmusic.com, as well as being a guest writer for her local newspaper.

J.A. McPhail now lives, writes, and sings Southern Gospel music with her husband, Dennis, and daughter, Stacie, in beautiful western North Carolina. But Kansas will always hold a special place in her heart.

About the Illustrator

Gwen Battis' love of art began in childhood when she regularly exchanged picture-laden correspondence with her equally artistic cousin. She is mostly self-taught, working with graphite pencil. As an adult, she began to incorporate colored pencils, watercolor and pastels.

Gwen worked as Assistant and Director of the very same Silver Lake Library where J.A. McPhail was director. After 10 years in Kansas and with their two sons in college, Gwen and her photographer husband, Rick, embarked on "The Great Adventure" of freelancing on the road, beginning with a fishing resort off the coast of Alaska and continuing to places they could hardly imagine.

Gwen's other works include the children's books, *Little Ike: Dwight D. Eisenhower's Abilene Boyhood* and the upcoming *Hark! I Hear a Meadowlark!* (available September 2012).